"Some wounds never really heal. We just cover them up and keep going."

"You think?"

Ross didn't answer. His arm was slung on the cushions of the sofa behind her back and Laurie slid a little closer to him. That warmth wasn't so confronting now.

"This is a little out of my remit, too." Clearly not too far, because Ross didn't move away.

"I think we're both very clear that you're not my doctor anymore."

He looked down at her, humor in his eyes. "Yeah, we've covered that one very comprehensively. You do, however, work at the clinic."

"And you're my boss." Laurie pursed her lips. "But I'm not on the clock at the moment. And this is nice."

"Yeah." He chuckled. "Maybe we make an exception, then."

She felt his arm around her shoulders and snuggled against him. No one could possibly have said for sure that this wasn't friendship and concern. If she disregarded her racing heartbeat and the cool scent of his body, then Laurie might almost believe it herself.

Dear Reader,

Around the time that I was planning this book, I was reminded about the first time I tried for publication. I sent my carefully typed pages off (on Valentine's Day!) and in return I received another first—my first rejection letter. Reading through my manuscript now, I'm in no doubt that this was the right decision, and the letter was encouraging enough to prompt me to try again, albeit many years later…

This first try occupies a special place in my heart, as do the book's hero, Ross, and its heroine, Laurie. So it seemed an appropriate gesture to name the hero and heroine of my latest book after them.

Even though the characters and the plot of this book owe nothing to the first, it was still a special pleasure to give this new Ross and Laurie the happy ending that I wanted for their namesakes. Thank you for reading their story!

Annie x

FALLING FOR THE BROODING DOC

ANNIE CLAYDON

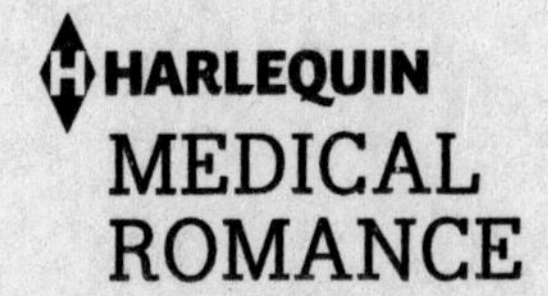

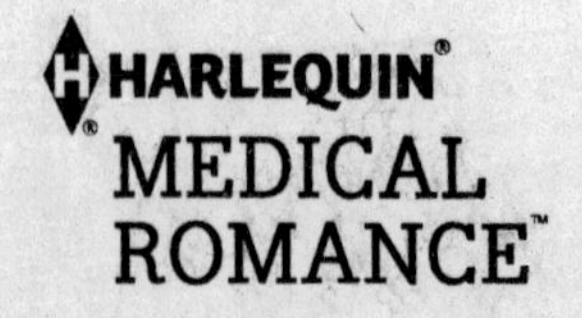

ISBN-13: 978-1-335-40867-9

Falling for the Brooding Doc

This edition published by arrangement with Harlequin Books S.A.

For questions and comments about the quality of this book, please contact us at CustomerService@Harlequin.com.

Harlequin Enterprises ULC
22 Adelaide St. West, 40th Floor
Toronto, Ontario M5H 4E3, Canada
www.Harlequin.com

Printed in U.S.A.

Cursed with a poor sense of direction and a propensity to read, **Annie Claydon** spent much of her childhood lost in books. A degree in English literature followed by a career in computing didn't lead directly to her perfect job—writing romance for Harlequin—but she has no regrets in taking the scenic route. She lives in London: a city where getting lost can be a joy.

Books by Annie Claydon

Harlequin Medical Romance

Dolphin Cove Vets

Healing the Vet's Heart

Pups that Make Miracles

Festive Fling with the Single Dad

London Heroes

Falling for Her Italian Billionaire
Second Chance with the Single Mom

Single Dad Docs

Resisting Her English Doc

Healed by the Single Dad Doc
From Doctor to Princess?
Firefighter's Christmas Baby
Best Friend to Royal Bride
Winning the Surgeon's Heart
A Rival to Steal Her Heart
The Best Man and the Bridesmaid
Greek Island Fling to Forever

Visit the Author Profile page
at Harlequin.com for more titles.

To aspiring writers everywhere.
Wishing you many happy endings!

Praise for
Annie Claydon

"A spellbinding contemporary medical romance that will keep readers riveted to the page, *Festive Fling with the Single Dad* is a highly enjoyable treat from Annie Claydon's immensely talented pen."

—*Goodreads*

CHAPTER ONE

DR ROSS SUMMERBY stood at the window of his office, staring out. The Lake District afforded many beautiful views, but this was one that he never tired of, the lake stretching off into the distance to meet mountains shrouded in morning mist. He frowned at the one blot on the landscape, a tiny figure in a small rowing boat, cutting through the still waters.

A knock sounded behind him and as he turned the door opened. Sam Kovak was clearly far too frustrated to wait for him to invite her in.

'Have you seen her?'

Ross nodded. 'Yep. Sit down, Sam.'

Sitting down didn't improve Sam's mood. It didn't much improve Ross's either, but as head of the Lakeside Sports Injury Clinic, he reckoned that part of his job was to listen to what everyone had to say, and provide a few calming answers if necessary. Sam looked in need of calming answers, and he didn't blame her.

'I told her specifically. No rowing. I've given her exercises to do that will maintain her fitness, without putting too much stress on her hip. What's not to understand about that? She's a doctor, for goodness' sake.'

'Doctors generally make the worst patients.' Ross grinned at Sam. 'Unlike physiotherapists, of course.'

'That goes without saying.' Sam puffed out a breath. 'So, as a doctor, what would *you* prescribe for another doctor who won't listen to her physiotherapist?'

'It's not you, Sam. She just doesn't listen, full stop. That's why I put her in your care, because if your unremitting good humour can't wear her down then I doubt anything else can.'

The remark mollified Sam a little. 'So what am I going to do? I've tried sympathetic understanding…'

Ross chuckled. 'And how did that work?'

'It didn't. She just rolled her eyes at me. So I tried reminding her—because I shouldn't need to explain—that bursitis of the hip will only get worse over time if you don't make long-term efforts to bring down the inflammation and restore muscle balance. Not only will she end her sporting career, but the hip will gradually deteriorate…' Sam puffed out a frustrated breath.

'What did she say to that?'

'Nothing! She nodded, and I thought perhaps I'd got through to her. Then I arrive here this morning and what do I see?' Sam gestured towards the window. 'It's almost as if she's determined to self-destruct.'

'Yeah. That thought occurred to me too. Leave it with me, Sam.'

'What are you going to do?'

'I'm going to give up on her.'

Sam frowned. 'I thought we never gave up on anyone. That's one of the things I like about working here, so don't tell me you're changing your policy all of a sudden.'

'Nothing's changed, I'm just making an exception. Maybe she's never had anyone give up on her before, and it's what she needs to make her face reality, eh?'

Ross had fetched them both a cup of tea, which was a way of calming his own mood as well as Sam's because Laurie Sullivan was beginning to get to him as well. A patient who had every chance of recovery but who seemed bent on destroying it seemed to mock all the people who'd fought against the odds here at the Lakeside Clinic.

As he walked out of the clinic, across the grass to the shore of the lake, he reminded himself that people came in all shapes and sizes. That no one should be dismissed because their actions seemed rash or not understandable. But Dr Sullivan was stubborn, and he was going to have to show her that he too could be inflexible when he wanted to.

He sat down on one of the wooden benches that were placed here for the purpose of enjoying the view. Laurie's rowing style was immaculate, as could be expected from a member of the England team, and Ross had noticed that there was a touch of grace about everything she did. It must have taken a great deal of work and determination to combine her impressive sporting achievements with a doctor's training, but somehow Laurie had managed it.

And now she seemed intent on throwing it all away. The one question in his mind was *why*? She was either too arrogant for words or there was something going on here that he had yet to fathom. This next conversation would settle that conundrum, at least.

It seemed that Laurie had exhibited enough defiance for one day, and she was pulling towards the small dock where the pleasure boats for those patients who *were* allowed on the water were moored. He'd wondered where she'd got the sleeker, sporting boat that she was using, and saw the flash of a boat rental company's logo at its prow. That must have taken a bit of planning as the boatyard was on the other side of the lake, a twenty-mile drive by road.

As she climbed out of the boat, Ross saw she was favouring her left leg. The stiffness in the right side of her hip hadn't been apparent when she'd been rowing, but that was no surprise. In his experience many sportspeople learned to work through pain to achieve excellence. Laurie caught sight of him and pulled off the blue woollen cap she was wearing to reveal her shock of red hair, cut short so that it wouldn't blow in her face when she was on the water.

She had the audacity to smile. There was a trace of mischief there, and somehow she managed to convey the idea that she expected him to understand that she may have bent the rules a little, but she'd done nothing wrong. As she walked towards him, she was clearly making an effort to hide the stiffness in her right leg.

She was perfect. Charming. And all this was about to stop.

'Lovely morning.' She stopped in front of him and Ross battled with the impulse to agree with her and allow her to go back to the clinic and get on with her day without any challenge.

'It is.' He motioned to the empty half of the long seat. That grace of hers, and her economy of movement, allowed her to disguise whatever pain she felt as she lowered herself onto the bench.

'Did you come out here to see me?' She scrunched her nose slightly. Great nose. The freckles gave it a lot of charm.

'Yes, I did.' Ross tore his attention from her face and got down to business. 'I'm discharging you.'

That provoked a reaction. One that wasn't carefully controlled to stop anyone from divining what she was actually thinking. Her face fell, and he saw a flare of panic in her golden eyes.

'You can't. I'm supposed to stay for seven weeks, and I've only been here a week.'

Ross nodded. 'I think we've done just about all we can do for you.'

Laurie thought for a moment. 'But…the consultant I saw thinks I should be here. I'm all paid up for seven weeks…'

That was the crux of the matter. The consultant who had referred her had told Ross that he'd been unable to pass Laurie as fit for selection to the England team this year, and her stubborn refusal to allow anyone else to tell her what to do about her injury had rubbed a lot of people up the wrong way. She'd be out of the team for good if she couldn't show her commitment to addressing the injury that had been troubling her for months.

'We'll refund you, of course.'

Ross felt the sudden urge to smile as he watched her trying to maintain her composure. She was doing rather well, considering the ramifications of what he was suggesting.

'I'm not…' She swallowed, as if about to admit to having murdered someone. 'My hip isn't…at full strength yet.'

She wasn't better. Despite all its success with much more intransigent injuries than Laurie's, the clinic had failed her. And this was the only way forward that Ross could see.

'Perhaps *discharge* isn't the right word. I'm throwing you out.'

This was embarrassing, and Ross's good looks weren't helping. Dark hair and melting brown eyes had always pushed all her buttons and he had a body that was clearly at home with movement and action. And the fact that *he* was here to deliver this message, rather than Sam, had the worrying implication that Ross meant business.

He had to know what he was doing to her, and that this place was her last resort if she wanted to save her sporting career. She had been such a fool, ignoring well-intentioned advice and allowing the situation to escalate like this. But she'd always had a problem with authority…

Those long years of training under her father's watchful eye had seen to that. Laurie had borne his insults silently, determined that he shouldn't see her cry when he called her a failure. Keeping going was all she knew how to do, and now she'd been given an ultimatum. If Ross Summerby didn't sign off on her stay here, then she could kiss goodbye to any hope of getting back onto the selection list to compete for her country.

Why? Why had she gone out rowing, in direct contravention of Sam's advice? Laurie couldn't even remember now why she'd thought that was a good idea.

'You can't.' Blind panic was gripping her, and it was hard enough to keep her face expressionless, let alone think of something more persuasive to say.

'I think you'll find that I can.' He was watching her closely, and she felt a shiver run down her spine. 'My difficulty is that we have a waiting list full of patients, all of whom are committed to their recovery. I can let you stay on for another six weeks, and we can pretend to treat you for your own convenience, or I give your place here to someone who we can make a difference for. What would you do?'

That wasn't fair. The answer was obvious. Laurie hung her head, looking down at her feet, the way she had when she'd wanted to hide her emotions from her father.

'I'm sorry. It won't happen again, I'll do everything that Sam tells me…'

'Maybe you will, for a little while. I'd give it a week. Tops.'

If they made a bet on it, then Ross would probably win. She looked up at him and saw a trace of sadness in his face. Kindness, too, in his dark eyes. He didn't like this any more than she did, and it gave her one last chance.

'Okay. You're probably right. Is there anything…*anything*…that I can do to change your mind and let me stay? If you throw me out now, that effectively ruins my chances of getting back onto the England team.' Honesty was her final resort. And it seemed to work, because Ross smiled.

'There is one thing. You may not like it very much.'

Laurie had already reckoned on that. 'That's okay. I can live with not liking it.'

'We have a small apartment that we use for visiting specialists. In the old building.' He gestured towards the large residential property that stood a little way away from the modern clinic building. 'You can stay there and make use of any of the clinic's facilities you want to, the gym and the pool. You can even book a session with Sam, as long as you're not planning on wasting her time by ignoring what she tells you.'

That didn't sound so bad. It was the kind of freedom that Laurie had wanted all along.

'But there's something I need in return.'

Maybe she'd let down her guard and her smile had given her away. Laurie turned the corners of her mouth down. 'In my experience, there's always a catch…'

'No one here gets a free ride, and I want you to work here, part time, for four afternoons a week. You can choose what you want to do. There's a pile of filing in our basement that needs attention. Or you could make use of your doctor's training. I have some patients that I think may benefit from your particular experience.'

Seriously? Laurie had started to think that Ross had thought everything through, but this was the most bizarre thing she'd ever heard. Filing didn't sound all that appealing and working here as a doctor was madness.

'You want me…a completely unknown

quantity…to work with your patients. You're sure about that, are you?'

His dark eyes softened suddenly. They were his greatest weapon, the one that made her heart pump ferociously and her instincts tell her that she could trust him. Her head was having trouble keeping all that under control.

'Sam tells me that a few of her patients have mentioned you've been encouraging them with their gym work and helping them pace themselves properly. Everyone here has some kind of stake in the clinic, and since you're no longer a patient then the only other option is employee.'

He let the thought float in the air between them. Ross clearly had few qualms about admitting his motives, but then he had nothing to lose.

'And it means you can keep an eye on me.' Laurie felt a trickle of embarrassment run up her spine.

'That thought did cross my mind. And I took the precaution of calling the director of the company that runs the chain of emergency GP clinics you work with this morning, and asking for a reference.'

'You did *what?* Thanks for that. Now I expect they think I'm about to leave. It's not easy to find a job in medicine that gives me the kind of time off that I need to train and compete…' Laurie bit her tongue.

'I imagine not. That's why I told her that I was considering asking you to help out here for the next six weeks, as part of your therapy, and that you'd be back with them after that. Adele thought it was a great idea and it would give you a chance to widen your experience a little. She put me through to your immediate boss and I'm sure you'll be pleased to hear that he gave you a shining reference.'

Laurie frowned. 'Adele. You know her, do you?'

'I know a lot of people. A clinic in an isolated location like this gets its referrals by going out and making itself known. And by being the best, of course.'

'You're sure about that? That you're the best?' Laurie knew that the Lakeside Clinic was the best of its kind, but she couldn't resist the dig.

'Yep. You're well acquainted with what it takes to be the best. Once you get there, you know it.' He leaned back in his seat, surveying the empty lake in front of him thoughtfully.

There was steel beneath that easygoing smile of his. He'd given Laurie exactly what she wanted and still she felt that he'd got exactly what *he* wanted out of the deal too.

'All right. Filing doesn't appeal all that much, but I have a good understanding of sports injuries and I think I can contribute something as part of your medical team. Are you going to pay me?' Maybe if the hours she worked came at a price, he wouldn't demand too much of her.

'Of course. I'm also going to be watching you, because our patients come first here. Always.'

That put her very firmly in her place. But Laurie could work with this. The ability to help others, along with the freedom to dictate her own regime, was what she'd always wanted. What she'd fought with her father for. If she disregarded Ross's watchful eyes, she could begin to persuade herself that this was going to be a piece of cake.

'You think I'd agree to work for you if you said anything different?'

'I wouldn't sign off on your working as a doctor here if *you* said anything different.' He gave her an innocent smile. 'Do we have a bargain?'

'You're saying that as if I have a choice. But, yes, it's a generous offer and it suits me.'

He shrugged. 'There's always a choice. I'm interested to know why you chose to row right past my window this morning when you could have quite easily gone in the other direction.'

Right. She should have expected that there was a catch to this. Apparently he felt their arrangement allowed him to ask awkward questions that she didn't know the answers to.

'No idea.'

'Maybe that's something we could talk about sometime…' Ross's smile was altogether too knowing, and much too delicious for Laurie's liking. She got to her feet, trying to ignore the stiffness in her hip.

'You can talk about it if you want. I'll pass…' She threw the words over her shoulder as she walked away.

CHAPTER TWO

THAT HAD…WORKED? Ross wasn't entirely sure whether he'd done just what Laurie was hoping he'd do, or she'd done exactly as he'd hoped. It was difficult to tell, but when he told Sam about the arrangement she nodded, professing her approval.

'You gave her no choice, then.'

'That's the part that bothers me, to be honest. It all feels a bit too much like blackmail.'

Sam rolled her eyes. 'This isn't a hotel, it's a clinic. The one thing you've always asked of everyone is that they're part of the community here. If we're at the point where there's only one option you're prepared to accept, that's because Laurie's shut all the others down herself. If this doesn't work, I don't see what will.'

'If it doesn't then I'm out of ideas. I really *will* have to think about throwing her out.'

Sam smirked at him. 'Of course you won't. You don't give up that easily, Ross.'

Nice to hear. Although he suspected that even Sam underestimated the extent of the problem. Laurie was tough, determined and it was almost impossible to read her. There was obviously something going on beneath that poker-faced exterior, but for the life of him he couldn't think what, and Ross suspected that getting to the bottom of it was the one way to help her heal.

That made honesty his guiding principle. Laurie was a doctor and, even if only half of her reference was accurate, an exceptionally good one. There would be no skimming over facts that she wasn't ready to hear, and it was apparent from their latest conversation that there would be no hiding *his* thinking behind anything. That was fine, but his growing fascination with her made everything challenging.

She was no less fascinating when he called into her room at the clinic to see when she'd be ready to move. Laurie was strikingly attractive, but didn't have the kind of soft prettiness that some found so appealing. The set of her jaw was a little too determined, and the look in her eye a little too challenging. She was the kind of woman that Ross could admire endlessly.

And she was ferociously organised. Her bags were already packed and she was ready to go.

When he reached for one of her suitcases she gave him a look that would have slain dragons and which sent tingles down his spine.

She fell into step next to him, wheeling both suitcases behind her, as they walked along the gravel path that led to the house. When Ross opened the main doors, she stepped into the entrance hall, looking around at the grand old staircase and the honey coloured oak panelling on the walls, which were in marked contrast to the clean lines and emphasis on light and space of the newer building that now housed the clinic.

'This is a bit different!'

Ross nodded. 'This is where the clinic started out.'

'Hmm.' She was taking in everything, the stained-glass panels in the doors, the flowers that Ross's mother kept in the hallway. 'When was that?'

'Thirty-two years ago. I was four, and my mother came here and started the practice, expanding it to a small clinic. We lived in an apartment on one side of the house and the clinic was on the other.'

'Thirty-six, then?' Laurie's half-smile told Ross that she was on a mission.

'I'll be thirty-six in a couple of months. September the fifth.' He threw the extra information in just to let her know that she could ask whatever she wanted about him. His life was an open book. Apart from a few pages that had got stuck together, but that was a long time ago now…

'And you were always destined to be a doctor? And come to work here?'

'Not really. I went through the usual cornucopia of career ambitions but in the end I decided that what I saw every day, the kind of good that my mother was doing, was what I really wanted. We'd never intended that I should join the practice, but she was ill for a while and I came back to help out. I found that this was where I wanted to be after all.'

'After all the time spent wanting to get away?' There was a hard edge to her tone suddenly.

'I wouldn't put it quite like that. I suppose you sometimes need to distance yourself from something for a while to realise it's what you really want. There's something to be said for feeling you have a choice.' Ross caught her gaze, and thought he saw a reaction in the fascinating depths of her eyes.

'Choices are what we make for ourselves.' She shrugged, looking around the hallway. 'You live here, then?'

'I have the apartment upstairs. My mother

has the one downstairs, and the guest apartment is at the back.' Ross began to walk towards the double doors that led to the single-storey extension, holding one side open for Laurie to manoeuvre her suitcases through.

'You live on your own?'

'Yes.'

'No partner, then?' She raised one eyebrow, as if that was difficult to believe.

Maybe these questions were intended to divert him from asking any of her. If she thought they'd make him baulk, she could think again.

'No. You?'

She shook her head. 'I travel light.'

'Yes I can see that.' He motioned towards the two large suitcases and she cracked a smile.

'I travel light in all other respects.'

Ross opened the door to the guest apartment and she walked inside, looking around. It was small but comfortable enough for a six-week stay and Laurie walked across to the windows, pulling back the drapes to let light stream in.

'This is lovely. You're sure it's all right for me to stay here?'

'Yes, it's fine.' He took the front door key from his keyring, handing it to her. 'It's all yours for the next six weeks. There's a small kitchenette, but you can eat in the clinic's restaurant. The cleaner comes in twice a week, Tuesdays and Fridays.'

Laurie smiled. 'They won't have much to do. I don't make a lot of mess.'

Ross had noticed that. Her room in the clinic had been impeccably tidy, with none of the usual bits and pieces that people brought with them for a long stay.

'I don't make a lot of noise either. I won't be disturbing you or your mother...'

'My mother's away on holiday for the next couple of weeks, and my apartment's upstairs on the other side of the building. Unless you're planning a rave, you won't disturb me.'

She shook her head. 'I don't have enough friends for a rave. The ones I do have tend to go to bed early so they can be up to train in the morning.'

He watched as she walked over to the French doors, unlocking them and stepping out onto the small paved area outside.

'Nice view. Aren't you worried it'll be too much temptation for me?'

'No. As I said, what you decide to do about your own treatment is entirely up to you. Are *you* worried?'

'I'll manage.' Laurie gestured towards the spiral staircase that ran up to the balcony outside his apartment windows. 'Do I need to turn a blind eye if I see someone sneaking up to your place?'

'Such as...?' Ross pretended he didn't know what she meant.

'I don't know. If you had a thing going with one of the women at the clinic you might want to keep it quiet. Or one of the guys...'

Ross grinned. When Laurie pushed, she pushed. He was beginning to like pushing back.

'All my guests use the front door. And, no, I don't have *a thing* going with any of my staff, and I'm not gay. You?'

'I don't have a thing going with any of your staff either. And I'm not gay. I'll call the police if I see anyone sneaking up there at the dead of night.'

'I'd appreciate it. Always good to have someone keeping an eye out.'

Ross wondered whether she'd like to come upstairs to his flat and take a look through his wardrobes. If he hadn't had a full schedule this afternoon, he would have been tempted to invite her up. But Laurie had already turned to walk back inside.

'If you're free tomorrow, I'd like to sit down with you for a couple of hours. Just to talk through which patients you'll be responsible for.'

She nodded. 'That's fine. But I'm going to

have to take a day trip back home before I start to work with them.'

Ross raised an eyebrow. Normally patients were encouraged to stay here at the clinic to promote a regular regime of rest and exercise. But then he'd just made it very clear that Laurie *wasn't* a patient any more, and he couldn't think of a reason why she should stay. Other than his growing curiosity, which wasn't anyone's business but his own.

'I need clothes.' She glanced down at the two large suitcases. 'Work clothes, that is.'

Right. Ross imagined that she would have noticed that the staff here often wore the same kind of casual sporting wear that he'd seen Laurie in for the last week. His own chinos and open-necked shirt were about as formal as things got. Perhaps there was another reason for her day trip, but he couldn't imagine what it could be.

'You'll be fine as you are.'

She shook her head. 'No, I have work clothes and sports clothes. The two don't overlap.'

It was a reason of sorts. And impossible to tell whether it disguised another motive.

'Okay, I've got to make a trip down to London the day after tomorrow to see some patients who've been referred to us. You want to join me?'

Laurie eyed him, a hint of amusement playing around her lips. 'Making sure I don't escape?'

Ross shook his head. 'You can leave any time you like, there's no need to escape. I'd just like to be the first to know if you do. Shall I book an extra train ticket?'

'Yes. Thanks.'

He'd either called her bluff or travelling down to London with him fitted in with her plans as well. Ross nodded his assent and turned, walking out of the guest apartment. He had no idea what Laurie was going to throw at him next, but he imagined that the next few weeks were going to be anything but dull.

What the blue blazes…? *Are you sleeping with someone at the clinic?* It was really none of her business. He could shapeshift into a vampire bat and hang upside down in the rafters all night if he wanted, it made no difference to what he did during the day as a doctor. Or as a boss. She supposed that Ross was her boss now.

One who had a very obvious interest in what drove her, and that was something that Laurie preferred to keep to herself because she wanted to forget about it. Her questions had started as a defence mechanism, a way of showing him how uncomfortable it was when someone else tried to pick your life apart, but he'd stubbornly refused to appear even slightly uneasy.

Then her own curiosity about him had taken over. Why someone like Ross didn't have potential partners queuing all the way up the steps of the fire escape. He had everything. Good looks, good job, a nice personality when he wasn't being so pushy. And even when he *was* being pushy he just oozed sex appeal. That wasn't her heart talking, it was a simple fact.

Laurie bent down to unzip one of her suitcases, feeling the stiffness catch in her hip. That was another thing. She'd fought so hard over the last months, trying to deny that anything serious was wrong, to both herself and everyone else. But Ross had taken that all away from her. He'd professed not to care whether she got well or not, although clearly he did. And then he'd put all the responsibility for her treatment squarely in her lap.

It was a case of being very careful what you wished for. Laurie had spent so many of her teenage years fighting for her freedom that it was a hard habit to break. She'd tried to free herself from being told what to do about her injury, and now she'd done it. It was a bitter victory, though, because she suddenly felt very alone.

Nonsense. That was nonsense. She'd feel better when she had work to do. In the meantime, she'd have to think about drawing up a therapy plan for herself…

At eight o' clock the following morning, Ross was sitting in his office, already working. Laurie wondered whether she should have come a little earlier.

Making a contest out of who could get up earliest would have been just petty. Juvenile. Seriously tempting, though. Laurie tapped on the frame of the open door and he looked up, beckoning to her to come in. Those eyes made the idea of competing with him even more enticing.

'Have you thought any more about which patients you might take on?' It was phrased as a question, but the curve of Ross's lips left Laurie in little doubt that he reckoned she had.

'I'd like to know a little more about what you're expecting me to do first.' She refused to think of this as her counterattack. It was just a query.

He leaned back in his seat. Ross was every inch the boss, relaxed and assured, with an elusive air of being in charge. He might like to pretend that there were options, but in truth his word was law around here. She could leave, but then she wouldn't get what she wanted.

'What do you think?' He batted the question back.

Laurie took a breath. 'I think that I could contribute medically, and in helping to structure exercise regimes, but then you already have good doctors and physiotherapists on your staff, so I'd just be another pair of hands. What you don't have are any professional sportspeople.'

He nodded. 'Go on.'

'I think that's unique experience that I can bring. I understand the pressures and how injury can be a challenge.'

'I agree.' He grinned suddenly. 'We see eye to eye so far.'

Meeting Ross's gaze was becoming the biggest challenge in all of this. She wanted to enjoy the warm tingle of excitement that it brought and smile back at him, but Laurie had to remember that Ross held her future in his hands. One of the lessons she'd learned from a childhood that she was largely glad to have left behind was that showing her feelings to an authority figure wasn't a good idea.

'In that case… I suppose that the choice of which patients I can work with most effectively is clear cut.' Best not name any names.

Best not give him the ammunition to slap her down, the way her father had.

'Yes and no. Pete Evans and Usha Khan are both professional athletes but…'

It was just as well she hadn't mentioned that Pete and Usha would be her first choice of patients to work with. It sounded as if Ross was about to rule them out. Laurie nodded and pushed two files across the desk towards her.

'I'd like to discuss two other patients with you. We're expecting Adam Hollier and Tamara Jones to join us within the next week, so you'd be able to take them on right from the start of their stay here.'

'That would be helpful.' Laurie reached for the folders. She'd never heard of either of them and wondered whether they were newcomers to their respective areas of sport. She flipped open the first file and ran her finger down the details for Tamara Jones.

'She's fifteen.' That was going to be a difficulty. In Laurie's own experience, fifteen meant traumatic choices and a lot of heartache.

'Yes. Tamara's a very promising young runner who lost the lower part of her leg in a car accident. She's had some problems with the fit of her prosthetic that have set her recovery back, and we're in the process of organising the adjustments. She's frustrated at the slow progress, though, and facing a crossroads in her life at the moment.'

'I can identify with that.' The words slipped out before Laurie could stop them.

'How's that?' Ross predictably picked up on every chance to ask her about herself.

'We're talking about Tamara. I can see that she's facing some enormous obstacles. How does she feel about the way forward?'

'The medical aspects of her rehab are just one part of the challenge. Tamara knows she wants to maintain her sporting activities, but the problems she's been having with her prosthetic have eroded her confidence.'

Laurie frowned. 'When you get that right she should find that she has a lot of options. Some runners who use blades are faster than those who don't.'

'In addition to what we can do for her medically, we'd like to help her explore all of those options. And help her get back to full fitness.'

Laurie closed the folder, clearing her throat. This young girl, trying to make the right choices in life, was uncomfortably close to home and tugging at her heart. She opened the next folder.

'Adam Hollier.' He was just a year older than Tamara.

'Adam's sustained a stress fracture to his

foot…' Ross stopped suddenly, looking at her as she felt her cheeks flame. Did he somehow know about her father, and the way he'd pushed her? Was Ross actively *trying* to break her down?

'Over-training?' She managed to get the two words out.

'There's no indication of that. As with Tamara, we need to address the medical issues, but also resolve how his injury has been caused. He's a bright kid and he knows that a susceptibility to this kind of injury may hamper him in the future, but he's so focussed on taking up sport as a profession that he can't see any alternatives.'

Laurie flipped the cover of the file shut. Slowly and deliberately, giving herself some time to think, she put the folders back onto Ross's desk. 'Can we take a break from this meeting? For a moment?'

'Sure. You want…coffee?' He took one look at Laurie's face and shrugged. Clearly he saw that she didn't.

'I want to ask you why you chose these two patients. Did you imagine that they'd be the most challenging for me? In which case, I think you should get your motives straight—you're here for them, not for me. We've already agreed that I'm going to take charge of my own treatment.'

He thought for a moment, obviously turning her words over in his mind. 'Honestly—'

Simmering anger came close to the boil. 'I find that being honest is always good. Particularly when you're dealing with a doctor-patient relationship and deciding whether the doctor in question has the resources to help a patient.'

'You're suggesting that this is all an experiment? That I've chosen a set of challenging patients for you and I'm going to stand back and see what happens?' His expression tightened into a dark frown. 'That couldn't be further from the truth. If you have issues that mean you're not able to help these kids, I expect you to say so.'

He'd boxed her into a corner. Or maybe Laurie had done that all by herself, but however she'd managed to get here she had to move. As she got to her feet, she felt pain shoot from her hip down into her leg, and almost stumbled. Ross started forward and she glared him back down into his seat.

'I think…' She wasn't entirely sure what she thought, but pacing seemed to help. 'Did you know that I was over-trained by my father? Well past the point of exhaustion at times. That I had to go to court in order to go and live with an aunt when I was fifteen?' It wasn't exactly a secret, the facts were a matter of record, and she'd been questioned about it more than once at press conferences.

'No, I didn't know that.' Something that looked like tenderness bloomed in his eyes, and Laurie ignored it.

'Well, it caused a lot of problems for me. Kids generally come with families, and I don't have much of an interest in trying to work out that kind of relationship. It's not my thing.'

'Fair enough. I'm not asking you to be a family counsellor, we already have a partnership with a very good one.' He paused for a moment, as if waiting to see whether Laurie was interested in that kind of counselling herself, and she bit back the temptation to tell him that there was a lake outside and he was welcome to go and jump in it.

'So what makes me the obvious choice for these two patients?'

'In my experience, teenagers come equipped with accurate radar. They know who really understands what they're going through, and they know who'll fight for them as well.'

'You're not trying to make my life easy, are you?'

He had the temerity to smile. 'Why would I? And if you believe that you can't help these kids, for whatever reason, we'll take another look at the list…'

Ross laid his hand on the pile of folders, pulling them back across his desk. In that moment a fierce protective flame ignited in her chest. Adam and Tamara were both facing a difficult and uncertain future, and Laurie knew how much that hurt. She really wanted to help them, and if Ross thought that she could…

'I didn't say that.' She walked back to his desk, grabbing the folders. She had to pull a little before he'd let go of them. 'I'll take them.'

'The meeting's back on again? That's your official answer?' A flicker of I-told-you-so humour danced in his eyes.

'Yes, it's official. I'll read through their histories and come back to you with some ideas. And unofficially…' She planted her hand on his desk, leaning towards him. 'You have a lot of good ideas, Ross. But you could try not to be so darned smug about them.'

Laurie didn't wait for him to answer. She marched from the room, hearing the door bang behind her.

CHAPTER THREE

WHEN A TAP sounded on the door, Ross wondered if it was Laurie coming back to make peace with him, and decided it probably wasn't. He was pretty sure that when Laurie banged anything shut behind her, it stayed shut. Then Sam popped her head around the door and he motioned for her to come in.

'Have you decided on annoyance therapy?'

'Um… Not sure. Ask me another.' Whatever Sam asked him was unlikely to be as challenging as Laurie's questions, or to ignite any flames of confused feelings.

'How about I just saw Laurie coming out of your office, looking like thunder and clutching some patient files to her chest as if she was going to punch anyone who tried to take them away from her?'

Good. That was good. The way she'd pulled the files from his grasp had told Ross he'd made the right decision. Laurie had something to give these kids and she knew it.

'We had a full and frank discussion.' The upshot of which had left a nagging doubt. 'Do I come across as smug?'

Sam had the grace to laugh at the idea. But then Sam always thought the best of everyone. 'Did Laurie say that?'

'She mentioned it.' The more Ross thought about it, the more it bothered him. He could take an insult, but Laurie had got under his skin and her opinion of him mattered rather more than it should.

'I've known you a long time, Ross. I remember when you were working to expand the clinic, and…dealing with other things.'

'You can say it, you know. I was there too, I know what happened.'

He'd come back here after qualifying as a doctor, newly married and with such hope for the future. Sam had been the clinic's first employee, taken on as the place had begun to grow, and it had been inevitable that she, Ross and Alice would all become friends.

Sam smiled. 'I saw how much you struggled when Alice left you. It was a hard blow for you, being told you'd never be able to have a family, and you worked through that disappointment. You built the clinic up, and made that your family instead.'

'Was it that obvious?' Ross *did* see the clinic as a replacement for the wife he'd lost and the children he couldn't have, but it still stung a bit when Sam said it.

'I knew what was going on because I knew both you and Alice. I don't think anyone else knew the details, but it wasn't so very difficult to see that you were in pain. If you seem a little...proud of yourself over the way the clinic's turned out, it's because there was a time when you had nothing else, and you put everything you had into it during those early years.'

Ross shot her a grin. 'Is that your way of saying that I *am* smug? Give it to me straight, Sam.'

'It's my way of saying that you could ease off a bit on Laurie. You're not her doctor any more and you don't need to pretend that your past has been all plain sailing. And, no, "smug" isn't the first word that comes to mind in describing you, Ross...'

Ross hadn't asked whether 'smug' was the second word that came to mind. Sam probably wouldn't have told him anyway as her approach generally consisted of dangling a few ideas and then allowing them to ferment. And this idea was fermenting at such speed he felt almost intoxicated by it.

He set aside the question of why this mattered to him so much. Why *Laurie* mattered to him. Why having her in the same room brought a tang of excitement, even if she was generally challenging him.

Ross had seen her from the window of the clinic, sitting in one of the wooden seats on the paved area outside the guest apartment, with a mess of papers on the table in front of her. He should go and make peace with her.

But there was no need. When he approached her, Laurie smiled. One of those radiant, mischievous smiles of hers, which couldn't possibly be anything other than genuine.

'May I sit?'

'Of course.' She waved him to a seat.

'I want to apologise.'

She wrinkled her nose. 'Really? I'd rather you didn't, because then I'd have to apologise back.'

He felt the muscles across his shoulders loosen suddenly. 'Then we'll put this morning behind us?'

She nodded. 'Since it's two o'clock, I think that goes without saying.'

Never let the sun go down on an argument. Ross dismissed the thoughts of all the nights he'd curled up on the couch when Alice had thrown something at him and shut him out of the bedroom. He should take Laurie's attitude for what it was and not make comparisons.

'I'd like to explain, though…' Laurie shook her head in a clear gesture that he didn't need to. Maybe not for her, but Ross wanted to for himself. 'Bear with me, eh?'

'If you want.'

'Setting this clinic up…was hard. I had to go out and find contacts who would refer patients here, and I was in the middle of a messy divorce. This place became my family and…if I'm a little too hands on at times that's something I probably need to work on.'

Her gaze searched his face. Laurie clearly wanted more, but Ross wouldn't give it. His decision to stay well clear of any potential romantic involvement had already taken a beating in the face of her golden eyes and indomitable spirit, and discussing the matter might only tempt him to change his mind.

'Maybe I'm a little hands off at times.' She gave him a grin that told him there was no *maybe* about it.

He wanted to tell her that she should never change. That her stubbornness was delightful when combined with her laughing honesty. But it was too great a step to take because it came from his heart, and his head told him that Laurie was still in danger of cutting off her nose to spite her face where her injury was concerned. *That* should be his one and only priority.

'Have you thought any more about your potential patients?'

'You mean the ones that you suggested, and who I'm not reckoning on letting you take away from me?' She stuck her chin out in an obvious challenge.

'Yeah. Those. I'm planning on going to see Adam tomorrow afternoon in London. It would be great if you have time to come along.'

'It'll only take half an hour to pack. And I'd like to come, it'll give me a start on getting to know him.'

Ross nodded. 'Tamara will be arriving the day after tomorrow.'

'Good. Are just two patients going to be enough to fill my time for four afternoons a week?'

'I'm hoping you'll be spending quite a bit of time with each of them. And if you do find yourself at a loose end, there are plenty of clinic activities you can get involved with.'

'Ah. Those would be the ones I haven't had anything to do with over the last week.' She shot him a wry smile.

'Yes. Those.' Ross smiled back. 'There are

a few outreach activities just for staff as well. We go to the Lakeside School sports day every year, that's a couple of weeks from now.'

'Okay… I've got to ask. What's your involvement with a school sports day?'

'We're part of a community here. We take an interest in what local schools and sports centres are doing and offer our advice and help on a pro bono basis, if they need it. The sports day is a good opportunity to go along and get to know people.'

Laurie nodded. 'That sounds like something I'd expect of you. Socially responsible.'

'It's actually a lot of fun. We dress up.' Ross had left the part that he reckoned Laurie might find the most challenging till last.

She shot him a sceptical look. 'Dressing up isn't really my thing.'

'Okay. Well you don't *have* to dress up, you can just come along. You'll be missing out, though, we've built up a few good costumes over the years. I usually go as the Mad Hatter.' Ross backed off from the idea and the effect was almost immediate. Laurie's lip began to curl in an expression of mischief.

'Where are these costumes?'

'We have them stored in one of the basement rooms. I can let you have the key if you're interested.'

'I'll do you a deal. I'll come in fancy dress if you let me choose *your* costume. The Mad Hatter doesn't really suit you.'

That sounded like a challenge. And Laurie's challenges were rapidly becoming both awkward and delicious.

'Yeah. I could probably do with a change. Why not?'

I'll dress up if you let me choose your costume. Laurie rolled her eyes at her own terrible judgement. That had to be one of the worst ideas she'd had in ages.

She watched Ross's retreat. When he walked away from her, she could stare, without risking being caught. There was a lot to admire about him, even from the back.

He was sucking her in. Into the life here at the clinic, the way everyone looked after everyone else as if it *was* an extended family. Tempting her to depend on him, to accept his judgement as sound. All the things that felt so hazardous.

She'd escaped the sticky tendrils of her own family. Escaped her father's heavy-handed attempts to control every aspect of her life, her training and her career. She couldn't give anyone control over her life like that again. Particularly not Ross, because it was so darned tempting to let him.

So she challenged him. Every time, and at every turn. Even that seemed to bring out the warm mischief in his eyes, and Laurie suspected that he didn't much mind. That was just as well because she wasn't going to stop any time soon.

If that meant choosing the most embarrassing costume she could find for him then so be it. It might be classed as petty, but it was a lifebelt in stormy seas, something to buoy her up and allow her the self-determination she'd fought so hard to attain.

CHAPTER FOUR

ROSS HAD BEEN wondering what Laurie was doing ever since their train had arrived at London Euston Station and they'd gone their separate ways. Whether she would really just go home or whether she had another secret agenda. Ross told himself that Laurie could have as many agendas as she liked, as long as she did the job he was paying her for, and worked towards healing her own injury. *Secret* was far too emotive a word, everything else was her own business.

The minicab drew up outside the small block of flats in London's docklands, at ten to two. The driver opened a newspaper, nodding abstractedly when Ross told him he might be a little while.

Being ten minutes early was just a matter of the London traffic being lighter than usual, but if he'd thought that he might catch Laurie unawares then he would have been disappointed.

She answered the door of her top floor flat wearing a pair of dark slacks and a white top, the neutral colours accentuating the vibrant red of her hair and her tawny eyes. It wasn't so very different from the attire he'd seen her in for the last week, but presumably this was what Laurie classed as her 'doctor clothes'.

It all became a little clearer when she beckoned him inside, asking him to wait in the living room while she checked that all the windows were closed before she left. There was an almost military neatness about the place, with none of the piles of books and mementos that adorned his own sitting room. Just space, and light, and everything in its own place. *This* was how she'd managed to juggle a career as a doctor with her sporting achievements, with the kind of ruthless organisation that made sense of having different clothes for her two different identities.

He walked over to the window. There was a magnificent view of St Katharine docks, with small boats moored by the old dockside and a couple of white sails scudding past in the distance.

'Tempting view, eh?' Her voice sounded close behind him, and Ross jumped.

'I can see why you like it. How long have you been here?' Ross wondered whether the tidiness might be just as the result of having just moved in.

'Six years. It's a very handy location as it's close to where I work, and my rowing club is nearby too.'

Ross nodded, trying not to scan the rest of the room for clues about Laurie's life. There wasn't much to be had from it anyway.

'You're ready to go, then?'

'Yes, all set.' She walked out into the hallway, grabbing her suitcase and ushering Ross out of the flat.

He'd deliberately not given Laurie any more details than the ones included in the file, wanting to see how she would handle her first meeting with Adam. The minicab drew up outside a comfortable semi-detached house and Laurie's suitcase was retrieved from the boot. Ross paid the driver and led the way up the front path.

'Dr Summerby. It's so nice of you to come.' Adam's mother, Ann, answered the door.

'Ross, please,' Ross reminded her as he stepped inside. 'This is Dr Sullivan, she'll be helping with Adam's treatment.'

'Also known as Laurie.' Laurie let go of her suitcase, leaning forward to shake Ann's hand. There was none of the suspicious caution that characterised all her interactions with the staff at the clinic, and the warmth of her smile left Ross in no doubt that it was genuine.

'Adam's in the conservatory.' Ann beckoned them to follow her. 'Still cultivating the grumpy teenager vibe, I'm afraid…' Ann lowered her voice.

Adam hadn't said much when Ross had seen him last, but he'd met grumpier teenagers. He heard Laurie chuckle.

'I'm told that grumpy teenagers of all ages are Ross's specialty.' She leaned towards Ann slightly as if confiding an important piece of information, then shot Ross a mischievous glance.

She was charming. Entrancing. And there was no doubt that her joke was partly aimed at herself.

'I've been known to have some success…' He glanced back at her, seeing a quirk of humour pull at her lips. Laurie was slowly picking his wits apart, leaving them in adoring shreds at her feet, and he made an effort to pull himself together.

'How does Adam feel about his injury?' Laurie turned her smile on Ann, who puffed out a despairing breath.

'It's difficult for him. He loves running and he's really good at it. Our other son is more academic, and this is the thing that Adam excels at.'

'You have a coach for him?'

'Yes, when he was little my husband read up on what you're supposed to do to encourage a child who's interested in sport and they used to go out for sessions together, but when Adam started getting really serious about his running, we enrolled him at the local athletics club and got him a proper coach.'

'And what's his coach's attitude to the injury?' It seemed that Laurie couldn't quite let go of the idea that Adam's coach had something to do with this. But it was a relevant question and Ross left Ann to answer.

'Sadie's been really supportive. I've shown her the diagnosis and she's done a lot to encourage Adam to follow all the advice that Ross has given. But Adam's pretty clued up about things and he says that no one can say whether this injury is the result of some weakness that will stop him from competing.'

'He's right.' Ross nodded. 'That's why we'd like to have him stay at the clinic for a couple of weeks, not just to help him recover but to help him work out how he's going to move forward from this.'

Ann nodded. 'We're so grateful you can take him. A cancellation, you said?'

'Yes, that's right.' Ross spoke quickly, before Laurie could react. He hadn't told her that Adam would be taking her place. 'I think that Laurie's own skill set, she's an athlete as well as a doctor, may be a good fit for Adam.'

'If he listens to anyone, he may well listen to you.' Ann gave Laurie a thoughtful look.

'I'll be doing my best for him.' The slight jut of her chin left no possibility of failure and that hurt unexpectedly. Ross had tried so hard to reach Laurie and she'd fought him all the way, but it seemed that Adam already merited her commitment.

When they walked into the conservatory, Adam was sitting in front of a large TV screen, obviously moved in there for that purpose, playing a computer game. His foot, encased in a supportive boot, was propped up in front of him. Ross hung back, holding a cautioning hand towards Ann. He wanted to see how Laurie would approach their patient.

'Hi, there. You're Adam? I'm Dr Laurie Sullivan, but I only answer to Laurie.'

Adam looked up at her, his concentration on the screen momentarily broken. Maybe he saw what Ross did, someone that he wanted to know better, because the controller slipped from his hand.

'Hi.'

'Switch that off, Adam...' Ann murmured the words, about to make for the screen, but Ross shook his head. Adam always did as he was told, but when Ross had last seen him he'd clearly not been enthused by the efforts being made on his behalf. He wanted to see if Laurie could change that.

'I'm working at the Lakeside Clinic for a while this summer.' Laurie's smile gave the impression that this was a bit of a holiday for her. 'I expect you'll be wanting to know why I think I can help you?'

It was different. Ross recognised the need to prove himself with each one of his patients, but he wasn't usually as forthright about it as Laurie was being now. But she seemed to have caught Adam's attention.

'Okay...'

'Right, then. Well... I'm a doctor, which you know already, of course. I'm also an athlete and I've had a few injuries in my time.'

Adam glanced at his right foot, looking away quickly as if it irked him. 'What injuries?'

'I broke my fingers once...' Laurie held up her hand, wiggling her two middle fingers. 'Got them caught in a rowlock. I made sure I didn't do that again. I couldn't hold an oar for ages afterwards.'

'You're a rower?'

'Yes, that's right.' Laurie's smile became even more luminous. 'I love it. I was at the World Championships last year.'

That got Adam's attention. 'What, rowing? For England?'

'I got silver in the women's single sculls.' She leaned forward towards Adam. 'It'll be gold next year...'

'I'd *love* to be able to compete at a national level...'

'Your sport's running?'

'Yeah, I was thinking of branching out a bit before I was injured.' Adam shrugged, as if that didn't matter any more.

Laurie nodded towards the game controller. 'Not the modern pentathlon? That was originally supposed to hone your battle skills...'

Adam got the joke, snorting with laughter. 'Nah. That's just a game. I was thinking more about the four hundred metres, instead of two...'

Adam and Laurie started to talk animatedly, and Ann finally smiled too.

'Looks as if you've brought your secret weapon along,' she murmured.

It did seem that way. Although Ross had had no idea that Laurie would manage to strike up such an instant rapport with the boy.

He dismissed the thought that everything she'd done so far seemed calculated to keep *him* at arm's length. That didn't matter. What mattered was that Laurie gave Adam what he needed, and in the process found healing herself. If Ross was to be consigned to the role of bystander, then so be it.

'You said that his teachers have sorted out some schoolwork for Adam to do while he's away. Perhaps we can go over the schedule together...?'

'Yes. Thanks. I'll make some tea.' Ann beckoned Ross into the kitchen.

It was hard to keep his mind from wandering away from what Ann was saying. Ross could hear Laurie laughing and talking, the note of enthusiasm dragging his attention away. Then silence, followed by the sound of the video game that Adam had been playing.

'Oh!' Ann looked up from the timetable in front of her, smiling. 'Is Laurie into video games?'

'Um... Not as far as I know.' Ross searched for any memory of a games console in her room at the clinic and came up blank. 'I'll admit it didn't occur to me to ask.'

'No, I dare say it's not the first thing you think of at a job interview. But Laurie certainly seems to be getting through to Adam, and these days that's a minor miracle.'

It was working. Ross had privately had his own reservations about the arrangement and Laurie had voiced hers in no uncertain terms. But if she saw what he did, then Laurie would have to come to the same conclusion that Ann had.

'Yes…gotcha!' He heard Laurie's voice from the other room. 'No! That was a sneaky move, Adam, how did you do that?'

He heard Adam laugh, explaining a bit more about the game to Laurie. Then the sound of electronic battle as they started to play again.

Ann was seeming a lot less worried about the prospect of her son being away from home for the next few weeks, and when they'd finalised the arrangements for Adam's schoolwork Ross accompanied her back into the conservatory.

'I'm sorry to drag you away…' He grinned at Laurie and she gave him a slightly sheepish look.

'Oh. Yes, of course.' She gave the games controller back to Adam and flashed him a smile. 'This isn't over, Adam. I'll get you next time…'

'In your dreams.' Adam was clearly looking

forward to the next time, and since that would be at the clinic, Ross was all for it.

'There's a bus that runs past the end of the road and goes straight to the station. If you can manage with your bags?' Ann looked at her watch. 'The traffic won't be too bad at this time in the afternoon.'

'Thanks. We'll manage.' Ross decided that he should take at least part of the responsibility for Laurie's large suitcase, and surprisingly enough he received a nod of assent.

As soon as they were out on the pavement, and Ann had shut the front door, she glanced up at him. 'Sorry. About the video game.'

'Really?' Ross shot her a sceptical look.

'Well…no, probably not. Adam's a competitive kid.'

And Laurie had given him something to compete with her over. The boy couldn't have missed her own fierce will to win.

'You play video games?'

She shrugged. 'No, not really. Never, in fact. But Adam does, so I guess I can learn. He says I can get a costume upgrade after I've played a few more rounds. That'll be a relief, my avatar looks like an entrant in a beauty contest at the moment.'

'And what do you get after you'd played a bit more?' Ross couldn't help but ask.

'Body armour. And a large sword...'

'Right.' He couldn't fight back the smile that accompanied the mental image of Laurie in body armour, her hair glinting in the sun. Twirling a large sword over her head. 'As you seem to be getting on with him so well, I'd like you to draft an exercise programme for him.'

'Great, thanks.' Laurie's eagerness to get involved was obvious. 'But that won't put Sam's nose out of joint, will it? She's an outstanding physiotherapist...'

'Yeah, I know she is. Sam's just pleased that she doesn't have to put up with you undermining all her good advice. She'll be fine.'

Ross wondered whether that wouldn't be a little too much honesty, but Laurie shot him a wry smile. 'I don't blame her. I'd feel exactly the same.'

She knew. And she seemed more comfortable with Ross's direct approach than Sam's kindly tact. When the bus came, she passed her suitcase up to him with only a minimal amount of protest, allowing him to lift it on board and tuck it into the storage compartment under the stairs. They made the earlier train with enough time to get coffee for the journey from the kiosk at the station.

Ross waited until the passengers were all seated, then settled himself into the seat opposite Laurie's, and the train pulled out of the station and began gathering speed.

He'd done exactly as he'd intended today. Laurie was becoming involved with the work of the clinic, and that involvement seemed to be tempering her approach to her own injury. Adam seemed to be looking forward to his stay at the clinic now, which was a great deal more than he had been. Mission accomplished. So why did this feel like a hollow victory?

Ross had begun to enjoy the challenge that was woven into their relationship, believing that maybe it was the way that Laurie interacted with everyone. But now he'd seen her with Adam, he'd realised that she *could* reach out to someone. It had led him to the inescapable conclusion that she just didn't want to reach out to him.

That was fine. It was okay. Laurie could do whatever she wanted to. Ross needed to take responsibility for his own feelings, and ask himself why it irked him so much.

He just needed to take one look at Laurie for the answer. She'd taken a book from her bag and was concentrating on the pages, unaware of his gaze. He'd been the odd one out most of his life, the friend at school who lived too far from town to be included in trips to the cinema or parties. For a few brief years, when he and

Alice had been together, he'd thought that he could finally belong, as part of a couple and then a family. That hadn't worked out and now he was the odd man at dinner parties, the table carefully arranged so that it wasn't too obvious. The one who went home alone.

He'd reconciled himself to that, and made the best of it. But Laurie had awakened the yearning for more, and he wanted her to notice him. Maybe even be a little bit special to her.

Ross opened his laptop, switching it on. It shouldn't happen, and if all the little reminders that it wasn't going to happen stung, he'd better just get used to it.

'Did you follow up with Ann? About Adam's trainer?'

Ross looked up from the article he was reading on his laptop. Laurie was still holding her book in front of her, and the question had come straight out of the blue.

'I did, as a matter of fact, while we were in the kitchen. She's sure that overtraining isn't the cause of his injury, the trainer's a friend of the family and she shares Ann's view that Adam should enjoy his sport and have time for other things.'

Laurie nodded. 'Okay.'

This clearly wasn't the end of the matter. Ross closed his laptop. 'You're not satisfied?'

She shrugged. 'I don't know. Kids cover things up. An adult always has that implied authority, and if the trainer *is* pushing him too hard, he might not say anything.'

'Or it might be that the trainer isn't pushing him.'

Laurie glowered at him, folding her arms and letting the book slide onto her lap. Something told Ross that this wasn't over, and he swallowed down the familiar rush of excitement.

'All right. Say it. You may as well, I know you're thinking it.' She was keeping her voice low so that other people in the carriage wouldn't hear her, but he was under no illusion that if they'd been alone she probably would have been on her feet and calling him out by now.

'I think that you may be looking for something that isn't there. Because of your own experience.' He murmured the words quietly.

'You might be right.' Laurie wrinkled her nose at the thought. 'And this is exactly *why* I thought that working with kids wasn't a good idea.'

'It's exactly why I think it is. You connected with Adam in a way I haven't managed to.

And you care about him, enough to explore every avenue.'

'I can't...' She shook her head. 'I *do* care. Maybe a bit too much, because I can't be impartial.'

'Okay. Let *me* be impartial. You be his advocate. As long as we both know where we stand, that's fine.' Ross sucked in a breath, knowing he was about to take a chance. 'Or you could decide that I'm wrong about all of this and you'd rather do the filing.'

At least she was thinking about it, not just firing back a knee-jerk reaction. Laurie pursed her lips.

'All right. I can be his advocate. Can we put that in the job description because I won't be giving you an inch if I feel you're not addressing his issues.'

'Be my guest. Since you don't *have* a job description, you may as well write your own. Along with your own treatment plan...'

What *was* he doing? Ross had never suggested that anyone write their own job description or treatment plan, but he had an idea that if he gave Laurie a little room she might just come up with something that was both innovative and brilliant. Taking a chance on her didn't seem any risk, as long as he watched her carefully.

'You'll be wanting to see them, though.' She eyed him charily.

'The job description… Yeah. I'll be needing to see that. I made it clear that the treatment plan is entirely your own responsibility.'

'I'm still not quite sure why you'd do that.'

Ross took a breath. This was demanding and exhausting, and yet somehow exhilarating. A little bit like the best sex imaginable, but that was *not* on his agenda. He'd stick to Laurie's issues with the paperwork.

'Have you thought about that stunt with the boat? Why you did it?'

She gave him that incredible enigmatic smile of hers. 'I'm sure you have a theory.'

'I do.'

'Then the least you could do is share it.' She tilted her jaw just enough to let him know that she wasn't going to be letting him get away with anything.

'I think that you spent your childhood being pushed far too hard. You must have learned how to question your father's authority, because you left.'

Her smile solidified on her face. Ross saw a flash of pain in Laurie's eyes, hidden quickly. 'Go on.'

'Even now, you're defying anyone who tells you what to do. Your consultant, Sam. Me, for sure. But there's a part of you that knows you need to stop, and that's why you rowed straight past my window.'

'You're saying that I'm undermining myself? That's a pretty smart trick. I'm not entirely sure I'm that clever.'

'Then you don't give yourself enough credit. And I think it's fair enough to say that most people have done exactly the same thing at some point in their lives.'

She nodded slowly. 'It's an interesting thought. Bit far-fetched, though, if you ask me.'

Sure it was. He'd seen the way that Laurie had reacted, and he'd touched a nerve. If she didn't want to admit it just yet, that was fine.

Before she could end the conversation, Ross pulled his laptop around, focussing on the screen. Out of the corner of his eye he saw her reach for her book again. Whatever she was thinking was hidden behind an impassive mask.

Why was he doing this? It was a great deal of trouble, and he'd have been perfectly justified in just discharging Laurie from the clinic, on the basis that she was refusing treatment. But there was no part of him that could let her go.

Not the lonely child who'd amused himself while his mother had worked all the hours she could to support them both after his father had left. Not the teenager, who'd spent much of his time alone, while his mother had worked. And not the husband, who had longed for a family of his own, but had been told that his chances of ever conceiving a child were somewhere south of one in a thousand.

His marriage hadn't survived, and he'd reconciled himself to the loss of his dreams, pouring all he had into the clinic. It had been his family when he'd been alone and hurting, and now it was Laurie's last chance. Ross wasn't going to let her lose it.

CHAPTER FIVE

SHE WAS BEGINNING to feel that Ross was far too perceptive. Deep down, Laurie had known that she was sabotaging herself when she manoeuvred right instead of left and had rowed straight past the windows of the clinic. But it had taken Ross to put that theory into words.

It was time to put her head down and work. Not to think about whether Ross was right or wrong, or any of the emotions he seemed to stir up so easily in her. She had aims. She wanted to get back to competitive fitness, and she wanted to help make a difference for Adam and Tamara. Ross wanted that, too, so where was the problem?

Wanting the same things as he did felt a little risky. She'd spent the last few days treating him as if he was the enemy, and if Laurie was honest she'd prefer it that he was. If he started wanting the same things as she did, they'd be tearing each other's clothes off before nightfall.

Not going to happen. Ross might seem to have his life sorted, but he'd dropped a few hints that had made her wonder whether he wasn't just as damaged as she was. And Laurie's own damage ran deep. Deep enough that she didn't want to re-create a family for herself when the one she'd had and left behind had almost crushed the soul out of her.

She got out of bed, almost stumbling as the morning stiffness robbed her hip and leg of their strength for a moment. A few stretches would sort that out, and then she'd go to the gym for her morning exercise routine. Then she'd concentrate on spending the whole day avoiding Ross as much as politely possible.

Stumbling block number one. When Laurie entered the gym she heard the muffled clank of weights from one of the machines. She reminded herself that there was no way that Ross could be checking up on her, because he'd been here first. Before she could bang the door closed behind her to alert him of her presence, he sat up, catching up a small towel and wiping his face.

Good definition. Really great definition. He wasn't muscle-bound but he was strong. Sweating. Laurie suppressed the urge to march over to him and ask him what he was doing here, because it really wasn't his fault that the male body held a particular allure for her when pumping weights.

'Hey. Just finishing up.' He got to his feet, obviously about to vacate the gym so that she could exercise alone.

'Don't rush away on my account.' She smiled, trying to inject a note of polite warmth into her tone that didn't sound too much like lust.

'I'm running a bit late anyway. I'll let you get on with...whatever you're about to do.'

His smile flashed an unmistakeable message. Ross had decided to back off. That was just as well, because when he passed her in the doorway she caught a hint of his scent. Raw sex, at its finest.

'Do you have a moment later? I've got a few questions about structuring the gym time for Adam.'

'Sure. Ten o' clock?' he called over his shoulder.

'That's great. Thanks.'

Stumbling block number two. How to stick to her routine when the clamour of pheromones was urging her to either fight or fly. Maybe some relaxation and breathing exercises were in order before she started on her morning workout.

* * *

It had been two days and Ross had kept his interactions with Laurie down to the bare minimum. She'd been working on her treatment plans for Adam and Tamara, and he'd left her to it. He'd skipped his morning workouts as well, so that there was no danger of his being there when Laurie went through her own exercise routine. He was aching with curiosity, and not sure how much longer he could keep this up.

But this morning she'd found her way to his office. The dark blue of her trousers matched her sleeveless top exactly, and she'd teamed that up with a pair of bright red sandals. He noticed that her fingernails were painted exactly the same shade as her shoes. He reminded himself that Laurie set store by dressing appropriately for any occasion, and that he was simply looking for clues, rather than appreciating the overall effect.

'Good morning. I was wondering if you had some time to see me today.'

Always. Particularly when she looked so good.

'Would now suit you? I was about to go and get some coffee. Would you like one?'

'Yes. Thanks.'

He fetched the coffee and found her waiting in his office, her laptop placed in front of her on his desk.

'What's your email address? I'll send my proposals through to you…' Clearly she just wanted to get down to business.

Ross reeled off his address and heard his computer chime. As he opened the document attached to his email a thought occurred to him.

'Have you chosen the costumes yet? Sports day is next Monday.'

'Ah, yes.' She smiled. 'I'm going as the chicken.'

The chicken costume was great. Covered in yellow feathers, and lots of fun. If Laurie had been looking for the most embarrassing costume in the clinic's collection, she'd chosen it for herself, but he imagined she'd carry it off beautifully.

'And me?' He tried to maintain an air of innocence.

'Not the Mad Hatter.' She glanced down at her hands. 'You're going as the egg. Or rather Humpty Dumpty.'

Right. As costumes went, the egg wasn't so bad. The kids had loved it last year when Mike had worn it, and it was difficult to feel awkward when you were almost entirely obscured from view inside a large papier-mâché egg. It was, however, a little difficult to go anywhere at a speed faster than walking pace, and the two eye-holes cut in the front didn't give a particularly wide field of vision. If Laurie had wanted to clip his wings, she'd done a fine job of it.

'Great. The chicken and the egg, then.' He refused to allow her to see his reservations. 'Who comes first?'

Laurie chuckled. 'We'll have to see about that, won't we?'

Three hours and two cups of coffee later, he'd been through Laurie's treatment strategies and they were very good. She'd obviously been talking more to Adam about his likes and dislikes and spoken to Tamara about what she wanted from her stay here. Ross had just one reservation.

'You've put a note here that you feel that Tamara might like to try rowing...'

'Yes.'

'What do you see as the specific benefits of that?'

'At the moment her prosthetic isn't fitting exactly right. I know you're doing something about that, but in the meantime it would be nice to get her moving.'

Ross thought hard. 'But rowing involves

flexing your legs. Tamara's prosthetic hurts her when she puts too much pressure on it, and we need to correct the imbalance that's causing. Won't rowing make it worse?'

'Yes, competitive rowing. I was thinking more in terms of a Sunday afternoon scull around on the lake. Just put some oars in her hands and see how she does with them.'

'That's fair enough.' Ross wondered whether Laurie was actually capable of taking a Sunday afternoon scull anywhere. He supposed he'd find out soon enough.

'But how do you get out onto the lake in the first place? You'll have to row her, won't you.'

Laurie shot him an exasperated glance. 'Look, I know what your reservations are. You think I'd do anything to get back out on the water and from your perspective…well, I can see how you might come to that conclusion.'

'So convince me.' Ross decided to give her a little more rope.

'You have excellent physios and doctors here and there's nothing I can add to what they can do for these kids. So I tried to think about something I could bring. My own unique selling point, if you like.'

'Go on…'

'For Adam, I want to bring an understanding of how frustrating it is to be injured, and how it can eat away at your own belief in yourself. And for Tamara… I just want to give her the feeling of power and speed that she once had when she was running and that she will have again.'

It was a different way of looking at the problem. But this was why he'd asked Laurie to do these treatment plans.

'Okay. I'll buy it. We can take Tamara out this afternoon if that's something she'd like to do.'

'We?' Laurie raised her eyebrow and Ross nodded. It was time to step forward again and be a bit more hands on, because he needed to know that this was really right for Tamara.

'If I come along, you won't have to do any rowing.'

She looked at him thoughtfully and then nodded. Maybe this last two days had convinced her that he wasn't simply meddling in her life for the sake of doing so.

'Okay. Can you row?'

'Not as well as you, but I've lived next to a lake for most of my life.'

She gave him a bright smile. 'I'll go and ask Tamara if she'd like to do that then, and come back to you. What time's good for you?'

'About three?'

'Great. I'll let you know.' Laurie snapped her

laptop shut, put it under her arm, and left his office without a backward glance. Ross was already looking forward to this afternoon, and hoping that Tamara would say yes.

He got to his feet, looking out at the lake. It had been his confidante as a boy, its ever-changing moods a source of endless fascination for him. When he'd come back here a newly qualified doctor, it had been the witness of bright new love, and then of disappointment and heartbreak. But now, staring out over the rippling expanse gave him no answers. Perhaps it had changed sides—those still waters knew that Laurie loved them and had allied themselves with her.

Nonsense. It was a large quantity of H2O, not a sentient being. He was on his own with the question of how he would convince Laurie that he really was on her side, and although he'd taken a first step, there was still a way to go.

Ross had voiced his reservations about this, but he hadn't turned the idea down flat. He seemed to be making an effort to give her some room and she appreciated that. She had asked Tamara about it carefully, not wanting to sway her with her own enthusiasm or her wish to show Ross that she was right. And Tamara had liked the idea and agreed. Laurie had lent her a windcheater and given the girl one of her favourite caps to wear, which bore the insignia of the England team.

They walked slowly down to the small jetty by the side of the lake, Ross helping Tamara over the uneven ground. Then together they guided her into the sturdy boat that would carry three with ease, and Tamara sat down in the stern.

'Okay, so watch carefully, Tamara. Ross is going to row us out a bit and then you can have a go.'

'All right. We're not going to sink, are we?'

Ross grinned at Tamara. 'Nah, we've got a professional on our team. I'm going to be following Laurie's instructions to the letter.'

The chance would be a fine thing. The thought of having Ross do exactly as she told him shimmered through her imagination, starting off with the professional and then branching out into what she might ask him to do by candlelight. It was an intriguing thought but probably better left for later, when she was back on dry land.

'Let's hope so, eh?' Laurie shot Tamara a mischievous look and the girl laughed.

The lighter oars for Tamara were stored in the bottom of the boat, and Ross sat on the bench between the heavier pair, swinging them out into the water.

'This feels a bit different…'

'Yes, I adjusted the oar outriggers. You're tall so you need them a little higher.' Laurie turned to Tamara. 'See how the oars are mounted on those triangular shaped brackets that stick out from the sides of the boat. That gives Ross better leverage, so we go faster.'

'Yeah, gotcha.'

'Right, then.' Laurie settled herself on the bench next to Tamara. 'Off we go.'

He started to row the boat out from the jetty. Three strokes, and then he stopped.

'What? You're looking at me as if I'm doing this all wrong.'

'No! You're doing fine.' She probably shouldn't interfere.

'I know you have a few thoughts about how I could do better, though.'

Laurie shot him an apologetic look and slid forward. 'Maybe put your feet a little closer in, then you've got room to bend your knees a bit more.'

'Like this?'

'Bit more…' Laurie shifted closer, gripping his leg and putting it in the right spot. Good calves. Very good… 'Back a little straighter.'

Ross squared his shoulders. Nice. 'How's that? Comfortable?'

He nodded, taking another few strokes with the oars and then stopping again.

'What now?'

Her face must have betrayed her. 'That's a great deal better. Only the ends of the oars should go a little higher in the water. You're not stirring a Christmas pudding.'

'You getting all that, Tamara?' He grinned broadly.

Laurie heard Tamara giggle behind her. At least she was enjoying this. And Ross seemed to be as well, so it was just Laurie who felt unaccountably nervous. She shifted back again, resuming her place in the stern.

'All right, then. Give it a go… Great. Good rhythm…' Laurie bit her tongue. That sounded like innuendo, but neither Ross or Tamara seemed to notice. Maybe it was just because a pair of good shoulders in action always turned her on.

'What do we do?' Tamara nudged her.

'We could sit here and trail our fingers in the water.' Laurie grinned. 'Let Ross do all the work.'

'No! I want to have a go.'

Ross shot her a smile. That was obviously the reaction he'd hoped for as well.

'All right. Watch how Ross is doing it for a minute. If he had a sliding seat, then he'd be powering his strokes from his legs and back, but with a fixed seat like that he's using his shoulders more. So you shouldn't need to push with your legs.'

'Right. So the prosthetic won't hurt?' Tamara pressed her lips together. Laurie knew that every step she took was painful at the moment.

'It shouldn't do, but honestly I don't know. We're trying things out at the moment, and we may need to adjust your seat and the outriggers before we get it exactly right, okay?'

Tamara nodded. 'Okay. Let's do it.'

She was so brave. Willing to try new things and looking at what she could do, not what she couldn't. Laurie wondered again whether Ross had deliberately chosen these kids to make her feel ashamed of herself. If so, he'd succeeded.

She helped Tamara forward onto the seat in front of Ross's, carefully shifting her own weight so that the movement didn't rock the boat. Pulling her own rowing gloves from her pocket, she gave them to Tamara.

'Put these on, it'll stop the oars from rubbing your hands. We don't want you getting blisters.'

Tamara pulled the gloves on, and Laurie fastened them for her at the wrists. Then she lifted the oars up from the bottom of the boat and fitted them into the rowlocks, before sliding back into her own seat.

'Try the movement a couple of times without dipping the oars into the water. Forward... now back... Good. That's very good. Are you comfortable doing that?'

Tamara nodded. 'Yes, that's fine.'

'All right. Let's give it a go, shall we? Try just one stroke.'

Tamara repeated the motion, dipping the oars into the water this time. The boat moved forward a little and she turned the corners of her mouth down.

'We didn't go very far.'

Laurie grinned. 'That's because you haven't built up any momentum yet. We'll try it again, yes? A few strokes this time.' She caught Ross's eye and he nodded. As Tamara pulled on her oars, he replicated the movement.

'See, that's better. Keep going... No, don't look round at Ross. It's my job to make sure he's doing it right...'

Laurie called out the strokes, and Tamara started to get into the swing of it. Ross was following her, and the boat began to move a little faster. 'That's really good. Well done. You okay, Tamara?'

'Yes. This is great!' Tamara was grinning broadly.

'Okay, I'm going to pick the speed up. Follow my count. Keep your back straight, Tamara...'

The two of them were rowing in perfect synchronisation now. Ross was doing more than his share of the work, but Tamara would still be feeling the resistance of the water against her oars, and the sensation of pushing forward. The boat started to move faster and she whooped with delight.

'Yay! I like this...'

'Keep your concentration... Good. Very good.'

They rowed in a more or less straight line, until they began to near the deeper waters at the middle of the lake. Laurie showed Tamara how to manoeuvre the boat around, and she managed it without too much help from Ross. When she began to look a little tired, they pulled for the shore.

'What do you think?' Laurie helped Tamara out of the boat.

'It's great. Can I do it again?'

Laurie glanced at Ross, and received a nod from him. 'As long as your leg's okay. Does it hurt?'

Tamara shook her head. 'No, it doesn't put any pressure on it.'

'I'll come and check on you later on, then. If everything's still fine, we can go out again next week. And in the meantime you can concentrate on your exercises so you'll be able to do a bit more.'

'Cool. I'm hungry…'

Ross chuckled, holding out his arm to steady Tamara over the rough ground at the side of the lake. 'We'll go down to the kitchen, shall we? Get them to make you a sandwich.'

CHAPTER SIX

LAURIE WAS WAITING for him in one of the small clusters of armchairs that stood in the deep window bays throughout the clinic. He'd have to come this way on his route back from the kitchen to his office.

Ross smiled when he saw her and flopped down in one of the seats. 'You're waiting for me to say it, aren't you?'

'I'm waiting to hear how Tamara is doing.' And to hear him say it.

'All right. So you don't want me to tell you that you were absolutely right.'

'I didn't say I didn't want you to...' Laurie smiled at him. 'Thanks.'

He heaved a deep breath of contentment at a job done well. 'And Tamara's in great shape. She's demolishing a sandwich and telling the cook all about her trip out onto the lake. Seems you may have a rower on your hands after all.'

'Not necessarily. But while she can't run,

it's good for her to have some goals. Ones that don't involve regaining what she had before. This is something different for her.'

'That's all?' He raised an eyebrow.

'I enjoyed it as well. Almost as much as if I'd been able to pull on the oars.'

'Maybe you will soon.'

Laurie puffed out a breath. 'You want *me* to say it?'

'Yeah. Go on. Since I shared first.' There was the hint of a tease in his tone.

'I've got an exercise regime and I'm sticking to it. Making sure I don't overdo things and stopping before I do too much. But then you knew that anyway, didn't you? Sam was in the gym the other day…' Laurie wondered how Ross would answer. She could understand it if he was keeping her under surveillance from afar.

'To be honest…?' Laurie nodded him on. 'No. I haven't asked and Sam hasn't mentioned it.'

She believed him. Maybe, after all the years spent looking over her shoulder, she wasn't so paranoid after all.

'My hip's feeling a little better.' Laurie turned down the corners of her mouth. 'Does Sam hate me?'

He let out an explosive laugh. 'Hate you? Sam doesn't hate anyone, she's one of the nicest people I know.'

'Yeah?' Laurie raised her eyebrows.

He rolled his eyes. 'What? I can't say something about one of my colleagues without you thinking I'm up to something? Sam's married with a three-year-old. Her husband's also one of the nicest people I know.'

'Sorry.' The inquisitiveness had gone too far. But Laurie had spent an inordinate amount of time wondering about Ross's love life. *You were right* had felt like a next step into intimacy with him, after long, battle-strewn foreplay. It didn't feel honest to engage in that if there was another woman in his life.

'That's okay. It's not as if the clinic's entirely immune to a bit of romance. Sam met Jamie here, he's an accountant and comes in to do the books for a couple of weeks every year.'

'That's...nice.' It sounded normal and happy and...all the things that Laurie's family wasn't.

Ross chuckled. 'Yeah, it is nice. They took one look at each other and suddenly Sam was interested in numbers. I think I gave her a pretty hard time about that, but she's forgiven me. Like I said, she's a good person.'

And life worked out for good people. What

did that make Laurie? Despite all her efforts to regulate her existence, to keep everything under control, her life was a mess at the moment.

'I guess it's all a matter of finding out what you want.' Laurie shrugged.

Suddenly, Ross's brow darkened. 'You think so?'

This wasn't about Sam or her husband any more. 'I think… I'm a sportswoman. Focus and working hard were my ways of getting where I wanted to be.'

'I don't underestimate those things.' There was a hint of regret in his voice. 'But I don't think life takes much notice of them sometimes. It's not always on our side.'

'You mean Adam and Tamara?' Surely Ross couldn't be referring to himself. He could take anything he wanted from life.

The moment's hesitation before he replied was his real answer. The clinic, his life here was one dream. But there was another that he'd lost.

'Yeah. Yeah, that's what I mean.'

She could ask. Laurie had the feeling that if she did, she wouldn't receive the head-on, honest reply that he'd given to all her other inappropriate questions. Ross had his secrets, the same as everyone else. And she should let them alone, they weren't her business.

'I ought to apologise to Sam. I didn't give her much of a chance, did I?'

He smiled suddenly. 'No, you didn't. And an apology isn't necessary. Although I'm sure she'd appreciate it.'

'I'll go and see if I can find her.' Laurie got to her feet and Ross chuckled.

'Don't waste a second in making it so, will you.'

He was teasing again, but she didn't mind. He made no move to follow her and when she looked back he seemed deep in thought. Laurie wondered if he was taking a moment out for the things in his own life that he hadn't been able to make so.

Life was getting easier now, just as long as Laurie didn't think about it too much. She was working with Tamara and Adam, and working with herself to improve the condition of her hip. Ross didn't ask about her own progress, but demanded regular reports on that of the two teenagers. Fair enough. Laurie couldn't complain that Ross didn't fully trust her yet when she was still wondering if she could trust him.

A taxi pulled up outside the house just as

Laurie was making her way back to the guest apartment, after a particularly gruelling session with Adam where he'd slaughtered her avatar twice. Laurie saw a woman get out and the taxi driver lifted two suitcases from the boot.

He might have stopped and helped her. But as soon as she'd paid him the driver got back into his car and drove away, leaving the woman standing at the bottom of the steep stone steps that led up to the front door. Laurie quickened her pace.

'Hi. Would you like a hand with those?'

'Ah, thank you. I thought I'd given him a big enough tip to encourage him to help me through the front door, but apparently not. I gave Ross a call from the car, though, and he'll be here in a minute.'

The woman smiled. Her dark hair was streaked with grey, but there was something about her eyes. Something about her wry humour, too, that reminded Laurie of Ross.

'Are you Dr Summerby?'

'I leave the Dr Summerby to Ross these days. I'm Maura.' The woman held out her hand giving Laurie's a firm shake.

'I'm Laurie… Laurie Sullivan.' This was awkward. Laurie wondered if Ross had told his mother that she was staying in their home.

'Ah, Laurie! Ross mentioned that you were

our guest for a few weeks. How nice to meet you.' Maura looked around at the path that led from the clinic. 'Where is he? I brought far too much back from my holiday, and these suitcases are heavy…'

'That's okay.' Laurie decided to leave the question of what Ross had or hadn't told his mother about her for later. 'I'm sure I can manage to get them up the steps.'

'Perhaps I should wait. He does like to lift things.' Maura's smile had all the warmth and mischief of Ross's. 'You know how men can be…'

Ross might be a man, but Laurie was a world-class rower, albeit a little out of shape. The competitive urge that told her that she didn't need Ross for anything took over.

'He might be busy. I'm sure I can manage.' Laurie lifted one of the suitcases, finding that it wasn't too heavy. 'Can you get the door?'

Maura produced her keys from her handbag, opening the front door for Laurie, and she heaved the case up the steps and into the hallway. 'If you want to wheel it through, I'll bring the other one.'

'Only if you're sure…'

Laurie nodded in reply, and Maura extended the handle of the suitcase, walking towards her own front door. The next suitcase was heavier, but she could do this herself.

The case was slightly bigger as well, and difficult to manoeuvre. Laurie managed five of the six steps, but as she took the last, pain shot down her leg. She lost her footing, tumbling down the steps, her arms slung instinctively around her head and her injured hip hitting the gravel hard.

Get up. Get. Up.

She wasn't sure if they were her father's words or her own. They were just words that had been with her since her earliest memories. She took a breath and sat up. When she put her hand to the gravel to help her get to her feet, it stung like crazy, but further inspection showed just a graze.

Get. Up.

Okay! What did the annoying voice think she was doing! Laurie gritted her teeth and got to her feet. Her hip was throbbing and she could feel blood running down her leg, but that was probably just a graze as well. She looked up at the top of the steps and saw that the case had fallen forward into the doorway. Just as well, if Maura had packed anything breakable in there.

The steps seemed like a long and lonely climb, when what she really wanted to do was sit down for a moment and get over the shock of falling. The fear that she'd just undone all the work of the past few weeks and had really hurt herself this time. But as she slowly made her way to the top of the steps, her hip didn't complain too much.

Maura appeared in the hallway. That was the last thing she needed right now. Actually, the second to last, the last thing being Ross.

'You've fallen…?' Maura's manner was suddenly businesslike. 'Sit down and let me look.'

'I'm all right.' Laurie forced a smile. 'Just lost my balance. I hope there was nothing breakable in your suitcase.'

Maura rolled her eyes. 'If there had been, the baggage handlers at the airport would have made sure it was already in pieces. Sit down and let me take a look at your hand.'

There was no point in arguing, Maura had flipped from new acquaintance to doctor mode. And it was a little easier to accept *this* Dr Summerby's help. If Maura just looked at Laurie's hand, and didn't mention the fall to Ross, maybe this whole episode wouldn't be so acutely embarrassing.

Laurie sat on the wooden settle in the hall, holding out her hand. Maura took her glasses from her handbag, looking at it carefully and then flexing her wrist.

'You've got a nasty graze there, but your wrist seems okay.' Maura was gently applying pressure in all the right places, and Laurie managed to smile.

'None of that hurts. I haven't broken anything.'

Maura gave a wry laugh. 'I dare say you could have told me if you had, I gather you're a doctor yourself. Although sometimes the shock of a fall masks injuries.'

'That's just what I'd be saying to you, if the boot were on the other foot.' Laurie couldn't help liking Maura. Her manner was a lot like Ross's, but she didn't have the annoying habit of questioning every answer that Laurie gave.

'Did you bang your head?'

'No. I landed with my arms up around it.'

Maura nodded. 'Good instincts. Come with me, and I'll make you a cup of tea and find a pair of tweezers to get those pieces of gravel out of your hand.'

Laurie was just searching for a way to refuse the offer when a dark shadow appeared in the doorway. 'Mum?'

Maura's face lit up at the sound of his voice. 'Ross, darling. I didn't need you to help me after all. Laurie came to the rescue with the bags. But she's taken a bit of a tumble…'

Laurie swallowed hard. Maura was obviously bent on salvaging what little pride Laurie had left, but from the look on his face, Ross wasn't buying it.

'Are you all right?'

'Yes. Fine.' Laurie tried to keep the curtness out of her tone. 'Really, I'm all right. Three doctors for one grazed hand is overkill.'

Ross was shaking his head, but Maura chuckled. 'I suppose so. It doesn't do to fight over a graze. Ross, carry my bag through, will you?'

He picked up the bag with irritating ease, his gaze still on Laurie as she got to her feet. Maura held out her arm in an indication that Laurie should accompany them through to her apartment.

'I'm sure you have lots to talk about. I'm going to leave you to it.' She shot a pleading look at Maura. 'Really, I'd rather see to myself.'

Maura's gaze searched her face for a moment. 'All right. I'll call in later to see how you are, and if you need anything, you know where I am.'

'Thanks. I really appreciate it.'

Maura nodded, turning to follow Ross, who had already disappeared towards her front door with the suitcase. Laurie breathed a sigh of relief. Maura would keep Ross busy for a while, and by that time she'd be back in the guest apartment with the door closed behind her.

Some hope. Her hands were still shaking from the fall, and as she willed the key into the apartment door, she heard footsteps behind her.

'I reckon if you really *were* all right, you could have managed a quicker getaway.'

Laurie closed her eyes. Apparently it was far too much to hope that Ross would stay out of this.

'It's not a getaway, Ross. And I *am* all right. How many times do I have to say it?' She didn't turn to face him.

'A tip for next time. The less you say it the more believable it sounds. Getting up and walking away doesn't make you all right either.'

She tried to choke it back, but the blind anger swamped all reason. 'Get *off* my case, Ross. I'm not your patient any more.'

'No, you're not. I'm sorry that you don't give me enough credit to expect I might show a little concern for anyone who fell all the way down the front steps.' He spoke quietly, but when Laurie turned she saw a pulse beating at the side of his jaw.

'I didn't fall *all—*'

His gesture of exasperation silenced her. 'The case was at the top, and you have gravel in your hand. It doesn't take a genius to work that one out, Laurie.'

‘I fell down, I got up. What more do you want from me?’ Suddenly her father’s demands seemed a lot less complicated. All he’d wanted was that she get up again when she fell. Ross wanted much, much more than that, and giving it went against everything she’d been taught.

He wouldn’t push his way into the apartment, that much she knew, and shutting the door on him would end this conversation. Laurie turned, groaning as pain shot through her hip and the keys jangled onto the floor.

She went to bend down but he was already in the way. Frustration and the shock of the fall were almost choking her. Even picking a bunch of keys up for her seemed too much to bear at the moment.

‘Get out of the way, Ross.’

‘Will you stop being so pig-headed, Laurie?’

As he straightened up, she saw the hurt on his face. Suddenly this didn’t seem fair and it occurred to Laurie that she was lashing out at the wrong person. Tears started to course down her face, and when he extended his arms she almost fell into them. He held her gently, silently, for what seemed like a long time.

‘I’m sorry. I’m not angry with you.’ Laurie felt his chest rise and then fall as she said the words.

'You should be. I haven't given you much room to breathe, have I?'

'It was my father that did that.'

'And then I made things worse. I knew that you had to stay here if you wanted to save your sporting career. It wasn't really a choice at all, you only had one option.'

'It was the right option.' Laurie wiped her face with her fingers, looking up at him.

He shook his head. 'I'm not entirely sure that makes any difference. I shouldn't have boxed you into a corner like that.'

'Make me a cup of tea, and you're forgiven. And give me a hug, because I fell right on my hip...' He knew what that meant. How scared she was.

His arms closed around her again, and she nestled against him. The first time anyone had ever hugged her when she'd fallen down. It was too short-lived, but maybe it was too much to ask for this one time to make up for all the others.

He opened the door, waiting for her to beckon him inside after her. Laurie fetched the first-aid kit from the kitchenette, putting it down on the coffee table and lowering herself onto the sofa.

'Tea first, eh?' Ross put the kettle on, watching as Laurie carefully rolled up the leg of her trousers. They hadn't ripped, but the force of the impact had left a red weal across her knee, which was oozing blood.

He brought the tea, and Laurie proffered her injured hand, knowing that he wouldn't ask to see the damage. Ross rotated her wrist, applying gentle pressure to all the same places that his mother had, but she let him do it. This was the beginning of trust, and it felt like a step away from the harsh regimes of her childhood. When he'd finished, she handed him the tweezers.

'Ow!'

'Sorry…' Each time he tweezed out one of the pieces of gravel that were embedded under her skin it seemed to hurt him more than it did her. 'That's the last one.'

'It's great. Thanks.' Laurie tried not to wince at the sting of the antiseptic as he gently cleaned her hand and then the weal on her leg.

'How's your hip feeling?'

'I'll have a bruise, but it doesn't feel too bad now. I don't think I've done any real damage.'

'Just had a bit of a fright.'

She nodded. 'Will you take a look?'

Ross smiled suddenly. 'I'm not your doctor, you know. Just an informed individual.'

'Maybe I'd just appreciate your opinion, eh?'

She rolled onto her side on the couch, feeling his touch through the thin fabric of her trousers, carefully working around the main areas of inflammation. 'I don't feel anything. In fact, there's a marked improvement on what I would have expected from your scans when you arrived.'

That was actually good to know. Her hip had been feeling better, but Laurie had been working blind, unable to examine it properly herself and loth to ask either Sam or Ross to do so.

'I may take a warm bath, just to ease everything a little.'

'Good idea. I'll go and let my mother know that you really are okay before she starts banging the door down to make sure.'

'Thanks. You'll come back?' Laurie didn't want him to go back to his own apartment just yet.

'Sure. It's fish and chips on the menu for tonight—would you like me to go and get a takeaway from the kitchen?'

'Sounds good. Have they got any tomato sauce?'

He got to his feet, smiling. 'I'll bring some.'

This was comfortable and reassuring and…all of the things that you wanted if you were feeling a little low. Someone to just take care of you, without going into all the details of why it was your fault that you got hurt in the first place, and how getting straight back up again would be the best thing to do.

Laurie had just slid into a pair of loose sweatpants, still warm and relaxed from her bath, when Ross arrived back with two large portions of fish and chips, along with condiments and a roll of fabric under one arm. She fetched two plates from the kitchenette and set about unwrapping their food.

'That's pretty.' Ross had unrolled the fabric and she could see now that it was a quilt, the central portion of which was a stylised rendering of what looked very much like this house, complete with trees and the lake.

'Mum sent it. She has loads of these, she's always liked to sew when she sits down in the evening. She reckons that handmade quilts are the best medicine when you're not feeling so good, so she sent one over for you.' He shrugged diffidently. 'Not a lot of medical basis there…'

'What do you mean? It sounds like solid reasoning to me.' There was the element of care in it, which everyone needed from time to time. 'Are you telling me that your mum's quilts didn't see you through a few childhood illnesses?'

Ross grinned suddenly. 'More than a few.

Some of my adult ones as well, although I don't admit to it. Not really needed in this weather, though.' He was clearly being careful not to push any unwanted concern onto her.

But it wasn't unwanted. Unfamiliar maybe, and Laurie had rejected it up till now because she hadn't known quite what to do with it. But it made sense of the way that Ross ran the clinic as a nurturing community. He'd learned all this when he'd been a child.

'Nonsense. It was really sweet of her to send it.' Laurie sat down on the sofa, spreading the quilt across her legs. It was a little warm, but it felt comforting to tuck it around her.

They started to eat. She should say something… Thank him, or tell him how much all this meant. She didn't have the words. It wasn't until Ross had cleared the plates away that she plucked up the courage.

'I'm…not very used to being looked after like this.' Ross had probably already gathered that. No one looked after people who had the kind of attitude that Laurie did.

He nodded. 'I'd worked that one out. The courts don't usually allow kids to decide who they want to live with, unless there's a good reason.'

'I didn't… It wasn't my fault…' She could

feel panic rising in her chest. 'My father said that I was making it all up, but I wasn't.'

The warmth in his gaze seemed to turn to fire as soon as it touched her skin. 'It never occurred to me that it *was* your fault. You want to tell me what really happened?'

Yes. Yes, she did.

'My father was a runner when he was young. He reckoned he'd stopped because of an injury, but now I think he just wasn't good enough. He always said that he'd been robbed of a good career in athletics and he wasn't going to allow the same to happen to his kids. He was very determined.'

'Living out his own aspirations through you?'

Laurie nodded. 'I think so. We got to pick our sports, my brother chose tennis and I chose rowing because I liked the water. But there was no room for failure, and no room for anything else either. I wanted to succeed, but I wanted to be a doctor as well.'

'And he didn't approve of that?' Ross's tone was even, but the flash of derision in his face showed how he really felt.

'No. I was supposed to move to part-time schooling when I was sixteen so that I could concentrate on my training. There was no time for anything other than sport, and…' Laurie shrugged. 'My aunt was very different from him, and she said I could go and live with her and stay on at school. She was the one who fought him and helped me leave.'

'Your advocate.' Ross's lips curved into a smile.

'Yes. She was the one person who really cared about what I wanted. If I can be half as good an advocate for Adam and Tamara...' Laurie shrugged.

'You're doing just fine.'

'Sometimes I wonder. There's only so much that a person can do to change. I tell Aunt Suzy that she's responsible for the best in me, but that my father had me for fifteen years. When I fell just now, the only thing I heard was his voice, shouting at me to get up. That was always his thing, you fell down and you got straight up again.'

'Which is the most ridiculous thing I've ever heard.' Ross's disdain sounded loud and clear in his voice. 'Getting up again is a matter of giving someone the support to do so.'

'Which is what you do here.'

He nodded. 'I can see how you might feel that's overly intrusive.'

Ross understood. She'd reached out and found that he'd been there all along. Laurie's heart did a back-flip in her chest.

'You said you had a brother?'

Two actually. But Laurie never talked about her older brother. Even now, it was too painful and she didn't know what to say.

'You've heard of the tennis player Ben Sullivan?'

'Yes, of course. He retired a couple of years ago, didn't he?'

'Shattered knee. Due to over-training probably. He stayed on with my father as his trainer, even after he had the opportunity to find someone else. He's a year younger than me. I didn't see him for a long time, he testified against me at my court hearing.'

'That must have really hurt.'

Laurie shrugged. 'There was a time when I would have done the same kind of thing myself, I wanted my father's approval so badly. I didn't speak to Ben for years, but when he retired he got in touch. He's living with his girlfriend now, and seems to have found some sense of normality.'

'Came to the same conclusion as you?'

'I think so. We don't talk about it much, there's a lot of hurt there still.'

'Some wounds never really heal. We just cover them up and keep going.'

'You think?'

Ross didn't answer. His arm was slung on

the cushions of the sofa, behind her back, and Laurie slid a little closer to him. That warmth wasn't so confronting now.

'This is a little out of my remit, too.' Clearly not too far, because Ross didn't move away.

'I think we're both very clear that you're not my doctor any more.'

He looked down at her, humour in his eyes. 'Yeah, we've covered that one very comprehensively. You do, however, work at the clinic.'

'And you're my boss.' Laurie pursed her lips. 'But I'm not on the clock at the moment. And this is nice.'

'Yeah.' He chuckled. 'Maybe we make an exception, then.'

She felt his arm around her shoulders and snuggled against him. No one could possibly have said for sure that this wasn't friendship and concern. If she disregarded her racing heartbeat and the cool scent of his body, Laurie might almost believe it herself.

CHAPTER SEVEN

IT HAD BEEN the first time in a very long time. Sitting, talking aimlessly, watching a bit of TV. Ross had almost forgotten what it felt like to have the warmth of a woman's body next to his. To feel cocooned in the quiet of the evening, knowing that someone else was there with him.

He'd been careful. Careful not to hug her goodnight or to kiss her although he'd wanted to do both very much. But something *had* happened last night. He'd known that Laurie's childhood must have been difficult, but not how much she'd been starved of the warmth that he took for granted. And in that understanding the first threads of trust had started to weave them together.

It wasn't enough. He couldn't allow himself to want more, because fate was both unpredictable and capricious in its cruelty. That was one thing he could never allow himself to trust.

She appeared in the doorway of his office

the following morning. He beckoned her inside, watching her movements carefully as she sat down.

'You're looking better.'

'I'm a little stiff, but there's no real damage done. Thanks for being a friend last night.'

Unless he was very much mistaken, that was a statement of intent. Laurie couldn't be unaware of the chemistry that fizzed between them, but she'd settle for friendship. It seemed that was something they could both handle.

'What can I do for you?'

'Sam said you were going into town this afternoon. Can you give me a lift?'

'Sure. I've got to get some things for the new mother and toddler exercise group. It's Sam's project, but she's pretty busy right now so I said I'd take over for a while.'

'Sounds good. I've heard these groups are very beneficial.'

'You want to help out?' Ross reckoned that he knew the answer to that already.

'No. It's not really my thing.' She smiled sweetly at him. 'I can help you shop, though.'

'I'll be leaving after lunch. Two o' clock?'

Laurie nodded, getting out of her seat. Ross couldn't help noting that she managed it without a grimace. 'Sounds good. I'll meet you at the house at two.'

* * *

She was there, leaning against his car, waiting for him, when Ross walked across from the clinic at five to two. Laurie seemed more relaxed in his company than ever, talking and laughing as he drove into town. Last night really *had* changed things.

'I just need to pop into my bank and sort a few things out. Then we can tackle Sam's list.' She took it for granted that they wouldn't split up and go their separate ways when they reached the large shopping precinct.

'Okay.' Ross sat down on the edge of a high brick planter. 'I'll wait here.'

She reappeared from the bank ten minutes later, and Ross led the way to the large mother and baby store. 'We should be able to get everything here.' He handed Laurie the list and she studied it carefully.

'Nappies? What are you doing, having them to stay overnight?'

Ross chuckled. 'No, Sam says that it's a good idea to have some supplies, in case of any emergencies.'

'Right. Well it looks as if she's expecting a few...' Laurie pulled a trolley from the stack by the doorway. 'We might be needing two of these.'

They walked along the aisles, stopping every

now and then to examine the toys on offer for Sam's toy box. Ross added a teddy bear to his trolley, which Laurie had picked up, and then a stuffed penguin.

'Oh, look!' She caught his arm. 'A baby gym. What do you reckon? We could phone Sam and ask…'

Ross walked over to the stack of boxes, running his fingers over the display model. 'It's well made, and it seems pretty sturdy.'

'But will they *like* it?'

'What, the mothers? Or the babies? Or Sam…?'

Laurie shrugged. 'I don't know. All of them. Perhaps we could ask someone.'

'Or we could make up our own minds.' That didn't seem so difficult. Ross came in here all the time to buy things for various godchildren and he always made his own decisions.

'Okay. You do that, because I'm not sure. I'll go and get some of the baby supplies, shall I?' Ross nodded, and handed her the list.

As he watched her walk away this seemed so different from all the other times he'd been in here, though. Laurie made all the difference. She was the woman he couldn't have, and here they were, buying supplies for babies that he couldn't have either. He stared at the baby gym. Suddenly it seemed to be mocking him.

He should pull himself together. But the pain was still as fresh as it had ever been. The moment he'd been told that he couldn't father a child. The times that Alice had thrown that into his face in anger, as if he could make any difference to the loss of all their hopes. The moment she'd walked out, saying that she was going to visit her parents, but taking six suitcases with her. He hadn't even had the chance to say goodbye properly, or to express his regret over what they'd both lost.

Laurie had stopped by the stacked shelves at the other end of the aisle, and was loading things into her trolley, consulting Sam's list as she did so. She was alone too, and maybe she could settle for a relationship that could never include any more than two people...

Maybe not. Laurie had made it clear that families weren't her thing, but people changed. It was a conflict that was impossible to resolve. His one great hope for Laurie was that one day she'd make peace with her own childhood and believe she could make a different kind of family. He couldn't hold onto that, and at the same time ask her to share a future with him that couldn't ever include a family.

He turned his attention back to the baby gym. He'd been over this in his head already, more than a thousand times. He should accept the way things were and get on with the matter at hand.

'Hey. What do you think?' He jumped when he heard Laurie's voice. Goodness only knew how long he'd been standing here, staring blankly at the gym.

'Oh. Um…not sure, still.'

'Are you okay?' She peered at him.

Not really. But it was one of life's rich ironies that there were occasions when the only thing possible was to fall down and then get up again.

'Yeah. Fine. I was thinking about something I forgot to do… It's okay, it'll wait until tomorrow.'

'Maybe you need a break, Ross.'

What he really needed a break from was this place. 'I guess I can ask Sam and come back another time.'

'Or we could just text her.' Laurie's gaze was searching his face.

'Okay. Do you mind doing that? I'll go and pay for the first trolley load and take it out to the car.'

'Good idea. That'll save a bit of time.'

* * *

Something was up. It was as if an invisible hammer had knocked Ross for six, and he was trying to piece his wits back together again. Laurie watched him go and then decided that the best thing she could do was to hurry up and get this shopping trip out of the way.

She texted Sam, who seemed to know exactly what she was talking about, and texted a *yes* back almost straight away. Then she grabbed one of the boxes, along with a few more stuffed toys, and made for the checkout. By the time Ross arrived back from the car, she was already halfway through the queue.

Something was definitely the matter. He was smiling and affable, but the smile seemed pasted on. She wondered whether he'd seen that in her when she'd been trying to avoid his questions.

'Are you hungry?' Sam looked at her watch as they finished packing the rest of their purchases into the car. 'It'll be nearly five o' clock when we get back to the clinic, so we could stop off for something to eat. My treat, since you got me fish and chips last night.'

Warmth flickered in his eyes. Maybe he realised that she was trying really hard to cheer him up. 'Yeah. There's a nice pub about halfway between here and the clinic. They have a garden at the back which looks out over the lake. If that's not too much of a temptation for you...'

'You can throw as many lakes as you like at me, I'm a glutton for temptation these days.' Laurie smiled up at him. 'I might even buy you a pint, and then drive you home.'

Ross grinned suddenly. 'Now *that's* an offer I can't refuse.'

The pub served great food, and they sat outside to eat. Ross's mood had improved, and he seemed in no hurry to get back to the clinic so Laurie suggested they take a walk.

'It really is beautiful here.' They strolled together by the side of the lake.

'Everything a woman could possibly want? Big empty stretches of water...'

He was teasing. But Laurie was fast coming to the conclusion that there was something she wanted a bit more from her stay here.

'Someone to talk about things to.'

Ross nodded. 'I'm glad you think so.'

She had to ask. He'd been there for her, and she wanted to be there for him. She didn't believe for one moment that his sudden change of mood had been anything as trivial as something he'd forgotten to do at the clinic.

'One thing I've learned is that the things

you feel that you can't say actually aren't so bad after all.'

'That's true.' He didn't take the bait.

'You've been here for me, Ross. I'd like to return the favour.'

He puffed out a breath. 'I'm sorry if I was a little short with you earlier. It's nothing…'

'I could throw your own words back at you, Ross, and remind you that the more you say that something's nothing, the less believable it sounds.'

'It's something.' Their pace had slowed to a crawl and he stopped suddenly, stuffing his hands into his pockets and gazing out over the water.

'Okay. That's all I wanted to know.'

She was lying, and Ross's sceptical glance told her that he was fully aware of that. Of course she wanted to know more, but pushing him wasn't going to help. He started to walk again, and she fell into step beside him. If he didn't want to talk, she should respect that. She'd fought hard enough to keep her own secrets. Just accept the afternoon for what it was and let him be.

He should let it go. Laurie didn't need to know about this, but he still wanted to tell her.

'I said that I was married. A long time ago…'

Laurie nodded.

'Alice and I met when I was at medical school. We got married and came back here, and then decided to stay. It was going to be the full turn of the circle for me. The lonely kid, who grew up and filled his house with children.'

'This seems like a good place to bring a family up.'

'Yeah, it seemed that way to us. We waited and nothing happened. After we'd been trying for a year we went for tests. It turned out that there is a one in a thousand chance of my ever becoming a father.'

She looked up at him, her eyes searching his face. Ross knew all the questions that were running through her mind, Laurie was a doctor, but she wasn't asking any of them.

'So I know you're wondering.' He turned the corners of his mouth down.

'Yes, I am. Sudden attack of tact.'

He couldn't help smiling, if only for a moment. 'There's nothing that medical science can do about it. I have a low sperm count that isn't linked to any other underlying conditions, it just means that I can't conceive a child.'

'And you were told a one in a thousand chance.' Laurie narrowed her eyes.

'Yeah. I explained to Alice that it's difficult for doctors to speak in certainties, and that one in a thousand was medical speak for *not going to happen*, but neither of us could stop thinking about that one chance. Each time it didn't happen, the disappointment got worse, but neither of us could bring ourselves to say 'never'. We tried IVF and that didn't work either. In the end she began to blame me for the loss that she felt. I guess that was fair enough, because it was my fault.'

'Your fault?' She was suddenly animated, and the fire in her eyes warmed him. 'I can't begin to understand what it might be like to be in that situation, but I do know that there's a difference between being the cause and being the culprit.'

'That's pretty hard to see when you're in the middle of it all.' He should give Alice the benefit of the doubt.

'I don't care if it's hard. It's the truth.'

He'd always known that Laurie spoke her mind, but Ross hadn't felt the full force of that before. It buoyed him up, relieving him of a little of the guilt that he felt.

'Sorry. That's just…what I think.'

'Don't be. I think it's what I needed to hear. Alice blamed me, and I just agreed with her.'

Laurie frowned. 'This is probably the wrong thing to ask, but…'

The weight lifted a little more. People generally didn't know what to say in the face of this kind of thing and so they backed off. Laurie was still there with him, and that was a precious thing.

'Ask it anyway.'

'Not everyone plans to have children.'

'May I ask *you* a personal question?'

Some of the tension left her brow. 'I really wish you would. At least I'll know what to say.'

The things left unsaid were the things that hurt the most. This was suddenly so very easy.

'What about you? Do you want children?'

Laurie gave the question some thought. 'My experience of families isn't one I'm keen to repeat, and if you'd asked me that a year ago I'd have said that I fought hard enough for my freedom and I'm not giving it up now. I still can't see it but…'

'But?'

'I guess never say never.' She looked up at him. 'Only you don't have that privilege, do you?'

She understood. 'No. I don't.'

Laurie took his arm 'I'm so sorry, Ross.'

The sudden hint of her scent, the feeling of

her skin brushing his made Ross recoil. Just that small, friendly gesture made him want to forget all that he knew to be right, and to want more. Laurie jerked away from him, as if he'd burned her.

'I'm sorry. I didn't mean…' He could see the hurt look in her eyes and there was only one way to show her what he really did mean. He reached out for her, taking her into his arms.

'This is what you meant?' She smiled up at him.

'Yeah. This too.' He brushed a kiss against her cheek.

'Mmm. I like what you're saying.' She stretched up, kissing his cheek.

A whole conversation would have been better. They were alone here, by the shore of the lake, and no one would ever know. Ross could feel his body hardening at the thought and wondered if she felt that too.

Maybe she did. But it was okay because everything was suddenly okay between them. Everything apart from the misunderstandings and the vain attempts to keep each other at arm's length.

'Are you going to say it again?' Her eyes were amber in the sunlight, her hair flaming. She was the most beautiful woman he'd ever seen.

'I shouldn't…'

She heaved a mock sigh. 'Yes, I know. You don't mess with your staff. Does it make a difference that I'm only part time?'

Ross chuckled. 'I'm not sure. It might come under the category of splitting hairs.'

Laurie grinned. 'That's better than a straight-out *no*. And remember that I've been in denial for much of my adult life, so I'm very good at it—'

She gasped as he stopped her talking with a kiss. One of the sweetest—no, *the* sweetest—he'd ever experienced. He could feel her fingers clutching at his shoulders, her body pressed against his. Her mouth, and the softness of her skin. When she responded, everything seemed to just fall into place and a bright happiness washed over Ross.

He told her that she was beautiful, and she sighed. Felt her run her fingers across his shoulders, and was suddenly grateful for all those mornings spent in the gym, because Laurie told him that she approved. Ross kissed her again, knowing that this was the last time.

'Time to go back now?' When he drew away from her, Laurie understood his meaning.

'There are only so many rules that we can break, Laurie. Too many of them and we'll end up hurting each other.'

She nodded, holding her hand out to take his. 'Then maybe we'll just walk very slowly back to the car...'

She'd kissed him. Twice. That was a breach of the rules of more than double the severity.

Because...once might be classed as a mistake, but twice definitely wasn't. When Ross had kissed her the second time it had felt as if the limits that they'd put on their lives weren't just wobbling a little, they'd been truly crushed.

All the same, she didn't want to take it back. Laurie couldn't bring herself to regret it either. What she should do was stop it from happening again.

When they came within sight of the car, he let go of her hand. Started to walk a little further from her, the quirk of his lips showing his regret. They both knew that they couldn't take this any further.

'As relationships go...' she smiled up at him '...that might have been short, but it was very sweet.'

Ross chuckled. 'Are you telling me that you're breaking up with me? Already?'

'Afraid so. But I really hope we can still be friends. Not just civilised, let's do this properly friends. Real friends.'

His eyes softened. 'That would be my fondest wish.'

CHAPTER EIGHT

This really shouldn't have worked. Ross had told his secrets, and Laurie hers. They'd kissed and then broken up within the space of half an hour. But somehow it did work. They were building something, learning how to trust and how to work together. And Ross had just learned that no one…*no one*…could carry off bright yellow feathers in quite the way that Laurie could.

'Ready to go?' He tried to keep his face straight as he saw her walking out of the front door of the house in her costume for the Lake-side School sports day.

She pulled the beaked mask up, propping it on top of her head. 'Yes, I think so. The feath-ers are fighting back…' She flapped one arm and a feather drifted upwards then floated back down again, settling on the gravel at their feet. 'Are you sure we shouldn't go for different costumes? When I chose these, I was trying to make a point.'

'Yeah?' Ross feigned innocence. 'What point was that?'

'Don't ask. It was a really bad idea. You really don't need to go as an egg.'

'Too late now. I'm rather looking forward to it. It's nice that you didn't go for any of the safe options.'

'I just hope you don't mind feathers in your car.' She wriggled suddenly in discomfort and turned her back on him. Ross busied himself with looking the other way.

'Ah, gotcha.' She turned, to face him again, still buttoning the front of her costume, and held up a feather, a triumphant look on her face. 'They get everywhere.'

'If you need a hand…' He probably shouldn't allow himself to smile when he said that.

'Trust me. You really don't want to know where they're ending up.'

He probably did. Ross dismissed the thought as unworthy of someone who was going to be dressing up as an egg.

He drove the few miles to the school, with Laurie sitting in the back seat, steadying the egg to stop it from rolling around, and showering feathers in the process. When he parked in the school car park she got out and tried to brush some of the feathers off the seat, only managing to replace them with a new set.

'Don't worry about that. Best to get all of them in one hit with the vacuum cleaner when we get back.' He took pity on her frustrated expression. 'It's probably because it hasn't been worn before. All the feathers that are a bit loose are dropping at once, and it'll stop in a minute.'

'You reckon so?' She flapped her arms again in a remarkable impression of a chicken. 'You might be right, it doesn't seem to be shedding as many now. Will you do me a favour?'

'Sure.' Anything as long as it didn't involve feathers inside her costume. Ross didn't trust himself with that, and having it turn X-rated in a school car park wasn't the image they were trying to promote.

'If I ever, *ever*, say that I'm going to choose costumes again, lock me up immediately.'

Ever. Again. It had a ring of friendship about it that warmed his heart. It was a very fine second-best option.

'It's a deal.' He reached into the car, carefully manoeuvring the egg out. It had a shock of painted hair at the top, a wide smile, and a pair of arms folded across its wide stomach. Below that, the yellow and black check that matched his trousers.

Laurie lifted the egg over his head for him, and he secured the shoulder straps that held it in place. It wobbled a bit when he took a step, but he could see straight ahead of him through the eye-holes. Only Laurie had disappeared…

'You all right in there?' He felt something brush his knee, and a feathered head appeared, peering up at him from the base of the egg. He chuckled, giving her a thumbs up, and she disappeared again, reappearing in his line of sight and pulling down the chicken mask over the top of her face.

They walked slowly over to the crowd that had formed at one end of the school sports field. He could hear Laurie's voice, a little muffled, talking to the kids who ran up to her and they both posed for photographs. He saw Sam doing the same in her blue and white Alice in Wonderland dress, while Jamie looked after their son Timothy. Laurie seemed to be slowly working her way over to them.

Sam waved, and he heard Laurie complimenting her on her costume. Then a blond head appeared at the bottom of the egg.

'Hey, there, Timothy.' He smiled down at his godson.

'Uncle Ross!' Timothy seemed to be intent on climbing up his legs, and there was just about enough room to lift him up in the confined space. The boy wriggled with glee at this amazing adventure, and Ross moved his head so that he could peer out of the eyeholes at his mother.

'Timothy!' He heard Sam's voice. 'Are you there?'

'Shh!' Ross pressed his finger against his lips and Timothy laughed loudly.

'Come out, come out wherever you are...' Sam's voice again, as she pretended to look around for her son, lifting the trailing tablecloth on the drinks table and looking underneath it.

'Where is he?' Laurie had joined in with the play-acting and was looking around as well. Thrilled with the idea of a talking chicken, Timothy shrieked, and Ross let him down so he could duck under the bottom of the egg.

'Here!' Timothy ran over to Laurie, and she squatted down, flapping her arms in a very good impression of a chicken. Sam was laughing, and Jamie rapped his knuckles on the side of the egg, shouting a hello.

The headmistress of the school, dressed in a nineteen-twenties flapper costume, came to welcome them, and the crowd of parents began to disperse towards the seating that was set up at one side of the large playing field. The children were shepherded by their teachers into groups, ready for the races to begin.

Laurie tapped on the side of his egg, presumably to attract his attention, although in truth Ross's attention had never left her. That was one of the advantages of coming as an egg, no one could see him stare. She led him over to the seating, and just as Ross was wondering how she was expecting him to sit down, he felt the egg lift a little. He ducked out from under it, and Laurie placed it on a seat and sat down next to it, her arm around it. Ross sat down on the empty seat on the other side.

'This is fun.' She was grinning out over the sun-drenched sports field.

'Wait till you start getting the questions.'

She turned to him, pulling the chicken mask up onto the top of her head. 'What questions? You never told me there were going to be questions.'

'I thought I'd save that as a surprise. I always get one or two questions from parents who've decided their seven-year-old is going to be the next world champion.'

She winced. 'You're not going to tell them, are you?'

'What, that you're a bona fide champion? They'd be fascinated…' He paused for a moment for effect. 'Nah. Don't think so.'

She fanned her face with her hand with an expression of relief. 'Just tell them that the best way to make a champion is give them a happy, healthy childhood.' She seemed to be wrestling with her costume, and was shedding feathers again.

'What are you doing?'

'Trying to get to my purse. That chilled lemonade on the drinks stall looks really nice. You want one?'

'Yes, but that's okay. I think Jo's heading our way.' He gestured towards the headmistress, who was walking towards them with two glasses of lemonade.

'Would you like to help give out the medals?' Jo proffered the lemonade.

'We get to give out medals? Yes, please,' Laurie answered before Ross could, and then frowned at the egg. 'Although I'm not sure how Ross is going to manage with his costume.'

'That's okay. You give them out, and I'll just tag along.'

'And the obstacle race?' Jo eyed the egg.

'I'll have a go.' Ross brushed Jo's reservations aside.

'I'd like to.' Laurie craned around the egg to look at him. 'My hip's fine. I can manage something like that. What do you reckon?'

Ross decided to ignore the fact that Laurie

had actually asked him what he thought, and answered for them both. 'Two for the obstacle race, Jo.'

'Righty. I'll call you when it's your turn.' Jo ticked the list on her clipboard and hurried away, brushing a yellow feather from her costume.

More feathers were dislodged during the course of the afternoon as Laurie got to her feet, cheering and clapping all the kids. All the children who competed got a medal, and when it was her turn to give them out, she presented each one of them as if it was a precious recognition of their achievement.

When she got to the little girl who was looking a little tearful, after having taken a tumble and come in last, Laurie presented her with her medal and then lifted her up in her arms. He turned to see Sam on her feet, cheering and clapping, and everyone else following suit.

'What did you tell her?' When Laurie helped him off with the egg, and they resumed their seats again, he saw the little girl run over to her parents, proudly showing off the medal that hung around her neck.

'I told her that it was a very special medal, because she'd been brave enough to get up and try again.'

Ross nodded. 'That's nice.'

And so unlike the woman who'd first walked into the clinic. She'd been quiet, self-contained and focussed. As if the only thing that mattered was winning, whatever she had to sacrifice in order to do it. Ross was proud of the fact that the clinic could work miracles, but this wasn't one of them. The Laurie who could give a child who'd come last in the race a medal and make her feel like a winner must have been there all the time. And entrancing as the old Laurie had been, this new one was downright irresistible.

CHAPTER NINE

Laurie's little joke had well and truly backfired on her. Two weeks ago she'd chosen the egg costume for Ross in an attempt to stop him from following her around to make sure she wasn't overdoing things. But so much had changed since then. And as it turned out, the yellow feathers were a bit more than she could handle, flying around everywhere and making her sneeze.

Ross glanced up and down the obstacle course, and then lifted the egg over his shoulders. Laurie put her chicken mask on, and they lined up with the others at the start of the course.

'What's he going to do about the skipping ropes?' Sam was in the next lane to Laurie.

'Goodness only knows. Improvise?'

Sam laughed. 'Yeah. We should finish as quickly as we can, so we can watch him.'

'Hey!' Ross's voice sounded from inside the egg. 'I heard that...'

Laurie rolled her eyes as the parent who had been given the starting pistol walked along the line to make sure everyone's toes were behind it. That was taking it all a bit too seriously. But as she looked down the course, she couldn't help feeling her heart beat a little faster. Couldn't help weighing up the opposition. Sam was the strongest of the bunch, and while Laurie was pretty confident she could beat her in normal circumstances, a chicken suit and a hip that shouldn't be overstressed would give Sam an advantage.

'Ready... Get set...' The starting pistol sounded and Laurie started to run. She and Sam got to the upturned gym benches, which were serving as balance beams, at the same time. Something was amusing the crowd, she could hear ripples of laughter.

'Oh, no!' She heard Sam's exclamation and looked round. Somehow the egg had got dislodged and Ross had become disorientated, veering blindly off course.

'I'll go and get him. You go.'

Sam hesitated.

'Go! You can still win. Honour of the clinic, eh?'

Sam grinned. 'Okay.' She jumped onto the

beam, making her way adroitly along it, just as the man who had just passed them overbalanced and stepped off his.

Laurie started to run back towards Ross. She couldn't believe she was doing this. Laurie Sullivan. The most focussed, competitive member of any team. She flung her arms around the egg, and Ross stilled suddenly.

'Who's that?'

'Laurie. Come along, it's this way…' She tried to adjust the egg so that he could see through the eye holes, but it wouldn't go all the way. That would have to do.

They made their way over to the beams, and once Ross found his he made a good job of traversing it. Then she ran for the slalom, checking that he was still with her.

'Crawl tube's next.'

'You're joking, aren't you?' She heard him chuckle. 'You go…'

From inside the plastic tunnel she could hear the crowd's reaction. Ross was obviously playing this for laughs, and when she emerged from the other end she saw him bending over to mimic an egg-shaped crawl. The skipping ropes were out of the question as well, but as she picked hers up and started to skip, he copied the motion with his legs.

Her father would have been screaming

his disapproval. All her life Laurie had been taught to compete, no matter what the context or whether the race was supposed to be fun. She'd left her father behind, but the guiding principle was so ingrained that it had turned into an instinctive reaction. Something she couldn't throw off.

But her father wasn't here. Ross was. There was a long straight run to the finish line, and she saw Sam at the other end, cheering and clapping. As Ross made his way at a slow canter, she ran behind him, stretching her arms out to make it look as if she was pushing him.

Everyone laughed. And the feeling was… Freedom. She felt free.

But as Ross made the finishing line, he tripped, staggering to one side and making a half-turn before he lost his balance completely. Laurie held out her hand to save him, but grabbing hold of a papier-mâché egg to stop the fall of a six-foot man was never going to work. He went down in a cloud of paper and dried glue, and Laurie only just managed to keep her footing.

'Ross! Are you okay?' She bent back the paper that was still covering his face.

'Yes. Yes, I'm fine. You didn't fall, did you?' The tenderness in his eyes was all-consuming.

People were crowding round, and she didn't even see them.

'No. Just managed to stop myself.'

'Coming through…' She heard Sam's voice. 'Coming *through*!'

A flash of blue satin on the grass beside her brought her to her senses. She could stay here on the grass with him for the rest of the afternoon, but that was sure to be remarked on by the teachers and the parents.

'Ross. Stay down.' Sam's put her hand out to stop him from sitting up and he ignored her completely.

'Too late.' Laurie shrugged. Ross was getting to his feet, brushing pieces of papier-mâché from his hair.

Sam puffed out a breath. 'Really, Ross. Laurie and I could have demonstrated all sorts of things to the kids. Neck braces, broken arms…'

'Dislocated shoulders.' Laurie grinned. She'd be very happy to inspect Ross thoroughly for bruises as well.

'Yes, dislocated shoulder.' Sam nodded sagely. 'That's a good one.'

'Sorry.' Ross chuckled. 'Looks as if the egg's the only casualty.'

'And the chicken.' Sam pulled the chicken mask out from under Laurie's knee, disturbing a small cloud of loose feathers as she did so. 'Think we'll get a gold medal for making the most mess?'

Ross nodded. 'Yeah. We came first on that one, at least.'

It was just as well that Laurie had thought to bring a pair of jeans along, in case she needed to change. Ross had fetched them from the car, along with his own change of clothes, and Laurie emerged from the changing tent with the remains of the chicken costume in a plastic rubbish bag, heartily glad to be rid of the feathers.

Ross was standing a few feet away, and the body language of the couple he was with screamed that now they had him in conversation, they weren't going to let him get away. He was nodding and listening, his smile fixed, and Laurie wondered whether she should go and rescue him. Then the man looked straight at her.

'Excuse me. Are you…?' He frowned, clicking his fingers as if he was trying to place her. 'The rower…'

No. She didn't want to be Laurie Sullivan the rower today. She'd been having too much fun. Ross turned and must have seen the dismay on her face.

'Laurie's on my medical team at the clinic.' He interjected quickly.

‘Ah. I could have sworn…’ The man frowned at her, and his wife shook her head.

‘Don’t, Brian.’

Okay. Maybe she *was* nothing like a winner today. Laurie gave a little shrug. ‘It’s okay. I get that a lot.’

‘About your son…’ Ross was steering the couple away now, and the thumbs-up gesture he made to Laurie behind his back told her that he had everything under control.

‘All the usual questions, I see.’ Laurie turned to find Jo, the headmistress, standing beside her.

‘Usual questions?’

Jo nodded. ‘Yes. Mr and Mrs Marshall have an older boy, nice lad, he’s in the senior school now. He’s very good at football, and when he was here they were very keen for me to get a special trainer along to the football club for him.’

‘He’s a little young for that, isn’t he?’ The children here were all aged from five to seven.

‘I thought so. But they wouldn’t listen so I called in my secret weapon.’ Jo smiled, nodding towards Ross. ‘Ross’s reputation meant that they accepted his advice a bit more readily.’

‘Not to be so pushy?’ Laurie wondered what her own teachers had thought of her father. What might have happened if someone had shown the good sense that Jo had, and had called in someone like Ross. Nothing, probably. Her father didn't listen to anyone.

'Football's a very lucrative career.' Jo mused. 'But at this age, our aim is to give pupils a broad range of basic skills that they can carry forward and that gives them choices. Ross has helped us to structure a good sports programme, and he's worked with a number of our children who have special needs. And he's very good with the odd pushy parent.'

'He understands the issues?' Maybe Ross understood *her* better than she'd thought.

'Yes. And he's very committed to giving the children a good start.'

'I thought…' Laurie smiled. 'I thought we were here just for fun.'

Jo laughed. 'Well, you are. But it doesn't do any harm to let the parents meet him in a less formal setting. I liked your double act on the obstacle course.'

Double act? Laurie wondered if her growing friendship with Ross was that apparent. But that had just been a bit of fun, too.

'Miss… Miss…' A little girl was tugging at Jo's dress and she shot Laurie an apologetic look.

'What is it, Lisa? I'm talking…'

'But Josh has fallen up a tree!'

Jo mouthed an apology to Laurie and squatted on her heels next to the child. 'Which tree, Lisa? Has Josh fallen *down*?'

'No. Up! Over the stream.'

None of that made any sense to Laurie, but it clearly did to Jo. She straightened up suddenly, looking around and waving to a couple to catch their attention.

'Run to Mum and Dad, Lisa. Now, please.'

As Lisa scampered away, Jo's face took on a look of urgent concern. 'Would you fetch Ross, please, Laurie? I'm going to see what's happened.'

Jo hurried away as fast as her heels would allow her on the grass. Laurie ran towards Ross, catching his arm to drag his attention away from the Marshalls.

'Jo needs you. Something about a kid falling up a tree by the stream?'

'What?' Ross apparently knew what that meant too, and he set off at a run, leaving the Marshalls staring open-mouthed after him.

'Sorry.' Laurie shot them an apologetic look. 'We'll be back...'

She followed Ross. He'd overtaken Jo, who was now running barefoot, and Laurie set her gaze on his back and ran, feeling her hip complain as she picked up speed. That wasn't important right now. Ross and Jo's reactions had left no room for doubt that something was badly wrong, and that a child was in danger.

Ross skirted the corner of the school building and Laurie followed him. Up ahead she could see a small knot of children pressed against a plastic mesh fence that bordered the edge of the school playing field. And beyond that…

A little boy seemed to be hanging upside down from the branch of a huge tree that overhung a stream. He was screaming, a mixture of fear and pain in his voice.

Ross had already reached the fence and was clearing the children to one side, looking up at the plastic mesh, obviously wondering if he could clamber up it. But the fence was obviously designed to deter climbers and afforded no footholds. Laurie put on a spurt of speed, and as she reached him he was bending down to the children.

'How did he get in?'

One little boy's hand shot up. 'He crawled under it. There.'

Ross looked round, and Laurie saw that the fence had been cut at the bottom. She might be able to wriggle through, but she doubted it. She bent down to try, but the hole was too small.

'That's not going to work…'

Ross knelt down, digging with his hands

at one side of the hole, and uncovering a steel spike that was driven into the ground, holding the bottom of the fence down. That would do it. If they could just free a bit more, they could get under. She started to dig on the other side of the hole.

'Steady. These are driven in pretty hard…' He gripped the curved top of the spike and heaved, expelling a grunt of effort as it came free.

His words didn't sting, the way they once would have. Laurie cleared the earth and found another spike, giving it a tentative pull. It was driven deep into the earth and it didn't move.

'Will you give this one a try?'

Ross grinned, but didn't say anything. He heaved the spike up, and Laurie set about uncovering a third one.

'Is that going to do it?'

Ross glanced at the fence. 'One more, on the other side. See if you can find it while I get this one up.'

Laurie cleared more earth while Ross concentrated on getting the spikes out of the ground. Jo had arrived, barefoot and gasping for breath, and was speaking into her phone as she herded the children away from the fence.

'Can you get under there?' Ross pulled the fence up as far as it would go, and Laurie wriggled underneath it. He was a tighter fit, and she had to put all her weight into pulling the edge of the fence out of the way.

The boy had seen them coming and was quieter now. Either that or he was beginning to suffer the effect of inversion asphyxia, but that would be unusual unless he'd been hanging there for hours. There was a tangle of ropes hanging from a large tree branch that hung over the river, and one of his feet was caught up in it. Ross was quickly taking in the situation.

'I'll wade out and see if I can reach him.'

'Yeah, okay. It looks as if I can get up the tree, but if the branch goes we're in a whole world of trouble.' The idea of the wide, heavy bough crashing down on top of both Ross and the boy didn't bear thinking about.

Ross nodded. 'I'll see what I can do from underneath first.'

He waded into the water, making his way towards the boy. The stream wasn't too deep, and he could reach the child's shoulders and support them, bringing his head up a little. But he couldn't reach his foot.

It was an easy scramble, up the sloping trunk of the tree. The huge branch that stretched out over the water was as steady as a rock, but she didn't put any weight on it. If the boy was okay where he was, it might be better to wait for the emergency services.

'What do you reckon, Ross? This branch isn't going to go anywhere.'

Ross's gaze flipped from the boy, lying listlessly in his arms, to the branch above his head. Laurie knew this was a difficult decision to make.

'We need to get him down now.'

'Okay. I'll slide out there.' She got down on her hands and knees to spread her weight a little, and crawled out. It was a journey of trust. Trust that Ross had read the situation right, and that they couldn't wait. His trust in her, that she'd take her weight off the branch if it seemed at all unstable.

The rope seemed to be caught in a complex arrangement of knots, and she couldn't see straight away which one would free the boy. But, stretching down, she could run her hand along the rope twisted around his ankle and find the right one. She tore at the knot, feeling her nails break and the warm, slipperiness of blood.

'Uh... Got it.' The knot unravelled and the tension of the ropes around the boy's ankle loosened, but his foot was still trapped.

'Can you get his shoe off, Ross?' Without

the heavy, thick-soled trainers his foot would slip through the gap.

'Can't reach. Can you manage it?'

'I think so. You've got him?'

'Yeah, he won't fall.'

There was a second mess of ropes around the branch. Laurie tugged at them and they held, and she looped one around her leg.

Carefully she edged forward, reaching for the boy's foot. Tugging at the hook and loop fastenings on his shoe, she eased it off. The boy's foot slipped through the gap in the rope, leaving his sock behind. When Laurie looked down, she saw Ross making for dry land, with the boy cradled in his arms.

Now she just had to make sure *she* didn't end up suspended upside down. The rope was holding her, but she'd had to shift forward until most of her body weight was over the water. She puffed out a breath, inching sideways until she was lying along the branch again. A moment to let her muscles recover from the strain, and then she unwrapped the rope from her leg and slithered down the trunk of the tree to the ground.

Ross had laid the boy carefully down on the grass, and was trying to gently rouse him. His eyes fluttered open but he seemed disoriented. That could be from shock, or the pain of his swollen ankle. Or it could be from some other injury as he'd fallen. Or from hanging upside down. Asphyxia caused by the internal organs pressing down on the lungs didn't usually happen this quickly but it was so unusual that there wasn't a lot written on the subject.

Ross was taking the most devastating of those possibilities first, and after checking his breathing, he pulled up the boy's T-shirt to see his back and chest and then applied gentle pressure to his ribs and stomach. No reaction. Laurie found the boy's pulse and nodded to him.

'No sign of internal bleeding.'

Laurie nodded. 'Let me check his hips and legs.' Children of this age were more prone to dislocations than adults.

Ross shifted to one side, turning his attention once more to rousing the boy. Laurie ran her hands carefully around his hips and down each leg. Apart from the swelling in his ankle, she could find no evidence of anything wrong.

'Hey… Josh. Open your eyes…' Ross had found the boy's name stitched into the back of his T-shirt. 'That's good. Can you take a deep breath for me?'

Josh took a breath. So far so good. 'My leg hurts.'

'Yeah, I know. We're taking care of that. Anything else?'

Josh shook his head. He was looking much less red in the face now, and more alert. When Laurie checked his pulse it was pretty much normal, which was probably more than could be said about hers.

A clatter at the gates in the fence made her look up, and she saw Jo unlocking them. She hurried towards them, kneeling down next to Josh. 'How is he?'

'We can't find any serious injury. But he needs to be checked out.'

'Okay. We have a stretcher coming from the medical room.'

Ross nodded. 'And his parents?'

'His mother's here somewhere, we're looking for her. Ah…here's the stretcher.' Jo seemed to have everything well under control.

The young teacher who'd brought the stretcher hurried off to fetch Ross's medical bag from his car. Josh was transferred to the stretcher, complaining loudly about his ankle, and carried into the school building. His mother arrived, looking anxious, and Laurie did her best to reassure her, encouraging her to comfort her son.

Ross didn't do anything by halves. His medical bag contained pretty much anything a doctor might need, and his examination was very thorough. Finally he was satisfied.

'Josh seems fine, apart from his ankle, Mrs Spencer. He'll need to get that X-rayed, though. He may have broken one of the small bones in his foot. I can give you a lift down to the paediatric accident and emergency department.'

Ross was erring on the side of caution, and Laurie didn't blame him. Josh's listlessness earlier had worried them both, and no doubt Ross would be reporting on that and the circumstances of his accident to the doctor at the hospital.

'Everything okay?' Josh had been seen almost immediately and Laurie had gone to wait in the car while Ross spoke to the A&E doctor. Jo had followed them down to the hospital so that she could take Josh and his mother home again afterwards.

'Yes, the doctor's pretty clued up. He's going to run a few tests just to make sure, but he agrees with us. The only thing wrong with Josh seems to be his ankle.' Ross leaned forward, his hand on the ignition key. 'Home?'

'I think we should. So far today, the only real casualty's been an egg, and I'd like to keep it that way.'

Ross nodded. 'Me too. I won't be sorry to get

into some dry clothes as well.' He indicated the damp patches on the legs of his jeans.

They drove in silence back to the clinic. Ross was obviously tired, but when Laurie took off her seat belt and got out of the car he called her back.

'Hey. Hope you didn't have too horrible an afternoon.'

'I got attacked by feathers, helped smash an egg and came last in a race. Then I helped save a child from a tree. What's not to like?' Most of all she'd loved being one half of the Ross and Laurie double act, which seemed to work equally well for the fun things as well as the deadly serious endeavours.

'Joint last.' He grinned at her. 'But I imagine even that was a first for you?'

'I think it must be. Consider yourself part of a new experience.'

Laurie heard him chuckle as she walked away.

CHAPTER TEN

Ross had taken a long, hot bath, and then walked over to the clinic. He'd done his evening rounds of patients and staff, and no one seemed to need him for anything so he'd gone to his office.

Laurie was perfect. Unstoppable. His own dreams had been put aside and had slept soundly for a long time now, and he'd been able to tell himself that his life here was all he wanted. But then Laurie's sense of fun, her determination to face down every challenge, was enough to rouse anything from the deepest sleep. And now the dream was coiled around his heart again like a serpent, squeezing hard.

It was crazy. He knew he couldn't have what he wanted, but he was unable to set it aside. The idea that they could overcome every obstacle and get to know each other a little better. Take their time, and then learn to build a life. A family.

A family was the one thing he couldn't give her. And that would destroy any life they'd managed to build. No amount of thinking his way out of this situation would change hard facts, so there was no point in considering the matter any more. Ross opened the folder on his desk that contained the outstanding paperwork for the clinic. He was a little behind, and he could spend the evening catching up.

Four hours later, he was done for the evening. But it seemed that the evening wasn't done with him. He paced his apartment restlessly, before resorting to the only place he knew that conferred a measure of calm. Pouring a splash of Scotch into a glass, he walked down the steps from his balcony and headed out across the grass to the lake.

It seemed that he'd been sitting there a long time on the small dock, staring out into the distance, when he heard footsteps behind him. No need to turn, he knew who it was. And even now he wanted her company. Laurie sat down beside him, swinging her legs back and forth over the water.

'Hey.' He turned to see her face, shining in the moonlight. 'You want some of this?'

'What is it?' She took the glass, sniffing at

its contents, and then took a sip. 'Mmm, that's good. Double malt. Not really enough for two, though.'

Ross shrugged. 'A little of the best is enough.'

'I guess so.' She took another sip and handed the glass back to him. When he brought it to his lips, he thought he could taste hers, but perhaps that was just his imagination.

They sat together quietly for a moment. It was nice. Companionable. Someone to share his thinking time with, if not his thoughts.

'So… I'm curious. Do you know what's going on with all the rope around that tree?'

'Um… Jo mentioned it to me the other day. The area of woodland is part of the school grounds, it's fenced off for safety reasons. Apparently there's some social media thing going on and they've had teenagers breaking in.'

'To wind rope around trees? I know that teenagers on social media have a mindset all of their own, but that sounds particularly odd.'

Ross handed the glass back to Laurie. 'It's a bit like bungee jumping. Only without the elasticity.'

'And they just hang there?'

'In pairs.' Ross was trying not to meet Laurie's gaze.

'What?' Laurie thought for a moment and

then started to laugh. 'They hang from trees, making out together? Is *that* what you're saying?'

'Yes.' He was glad she'd put it into words so that he didn't have to. 'Jo said she found a few used condoms at the side of the river the other day. She's worried about it, of course. The school uses that land to teach the kids about wildlife and caring for woodlands, so they use it pretty regularly. I imagine they tried to cut the fence, where we found that hole, and discovered it was too tough so they got in another way. The hole wasn't big enough for an adult to get through, but a child could manage it.'

'Have you had anything like that on the clinic's land?'

'No, thank goodness. There's always someone wandering around, day or night, so they're a lot more likely to be seen. Or maybe we just don't have the right kind of tree.'

'Mmm. You'd need height and a really strong, unobstructed branch. Do you think the water's one of the essential requirements?'

'Don't...' Ross shook his head. 'Don't even try to work it out. You won't be able to unthink it later.'

'I half wish I could have done something a little crazy when I was a teenager.' Ross shot

Laurie a questioning look and she grinned. 'Not *that* crazy. Just being allowed to have a boyfriend would have been nice.'

'Too busy training?'

She nodded. 'Yeah. Everything was about the training. Or maybe everything was just about my father, and he was all about the training. What about you? You must have found a few things to get up to around here. All this countryside and the lakes.'

Ross couldn't think of anything. 'Not really. A four-mile bike ride each way to the nearest town tends to put the lid on too much impromptu mischief-making. That's one of the disadvantages of living in such a secluded place. Although my mother might say it was an advantage.'

'So we were both lonely.' She took a sip from the glass and gave it back to him.

'I have the clinic. You have...' Laurie had a future, and he could see her moving forward to grasp it with both hands.

'A dodgy hip and a capacity for denial?' She chuckled.

'Your hip's on the mend. You're going to be back in a boat soon, and getting ready to win that gold medal.' Ross didn't want to think about all the other things that Laurie could do, because they wouldn't be with him.

'I have faith in you.' She turned suddenly to face him, her skin pale in the darkness.

Was that enough? He wanted it to be, but it wasn't.

'I have faith in you, too. I just don't have much faith in the future any more.'

Laurie's hand moved to the side of his face, her fingers resting lightly on his cheek. 'I wish you would, Ross. If you did, then maybe we—'

He laid his finger across her lips. Ross didn't want to hear about all the things that Laurie thought they could do together, because they were impossible.

'That's the difference between us, Laurie. You can change your future. I can't change mine.'

She flung her arms around his neck, as if she could somehow save him from something. Then suddenly she jumped away from him, her hand flying to her mouth.

'That's embarrassing, isn't it? Hugging the boss in front of everyone.'

'Look around. This happens to be the one place that isn't visible from any of the clinic windows.'

She looked, and then gave him a smile. 'I'm so glad you knew that. It smacks of a little healthy misbehaviour. You're beginning to seem quite human to me.'

'Thanks!' He feigned outrage. 'I didn't seem human before?'

'You're right a little too often for my liking.'

'I can be wrong...' He wanted so badly to be wrong. Wrong about everything, his sure knowledge that taking things further with Laurie would end in catastrophe.

And then there were those eyes. Dark and knowing. The hand that caressed the side of his face sending shivers down his spine. Ross leaned forward, planting a kiss on her cheek.

'What was it you said? A little of the best is enough?' She murmured the words. So close now that they were almost touching, and he could feel her breath on his cheek.

His fingertips grazed her arm. Her leg pressed against his. Each moment, each touch was precious and exquisite. And then one rush of emotion as he put his arms around her and kissed her. Her response matched his. Audacious and hungry, as if the past didn't exist and the future hadn't happened yet. Taking each moment, without fear or regret.

'That was undoubtedly the best thing that didn't happen to me today.' He held her close, knowing he'd have to let her go soon.

She reached up, running her thumb across his lips. 'I suppose if it never happened, then we could do it again...'

* * *

Laurie had asked for the day off today. That wasn't unexpected, she'd worked far more hours than she was being paid for over the last couple of weeks, and maybe she had other things to do. But Ross missed seeing her around the clinic.

When he'd popped into Adam's room, on his daily round of patients and staff, the boy had said that Laurie wouldn't be coming to play computer games with him today, even though she'd amassed enough points to give her avatar a complete change of wardrobe. She wasn't in the lounge, or walking by the side of the lake. And unless Ross was very much mistaken, she wouldn't be out in a boat somewhere.

Or would she? It had been almost three weeks since he'd seen her rowing past his window, and he knew that she missed it. Maybe that wayward spirit of hers had just had enough of the clinic's calm, ordered existence and she'd decided she needed to get back into a boat. He'd made it clear that he was no longer responsible for her treatment, but the thought still bothered him.

She hadn't taken one of the clinic's electric cars into town, and when Ross found an excuse to pop back to his flat for something, he noticed that the long curtains in the living room of the small apartment downstairs were drawn, even though it was nearly lunchtime. It was odd, because Laurie was such a creature of the light. She loved it and it loved her.

He'd told her that he trusted her, and he'd made a promise. He should keep it. She just wanted a day to herself and he shouldn't interrupt…

Ross arrived home late after an evening spent at the clinic, and opened the French doors that led out onto the balcony. As he stared out over the dark water of the lake, he saw a figure sitting on the bench at the water's edge. Laurie.

What was she doing down there? It was a warm evening, and the calm of the lake often drew him to that spot, but there was something about the way she was sitting, her shoulders hunched and her head bowed. Without even thinking about whether it was a good idea or not, he took the steps down from the balcony two at a time and walked down to the lake.

She must have heard his footsteps on the uneven ground because she turned her head towards him. He could see her face now, pale and impassive in the twilight, and she was nursing something on her lap.

'Hey…' Some instinct stopped him from remarking on the warmth of the evening. This didn't seem the right time for pleasantries.

'Hi, Ross.'

'May I join you?'

She nodded, as if she didn't much care either way, and Ross sat down on the bench. He could see now what she was holding—a small wooden model of a boat.

'What's going on?'

Laurie puffed out a breath. 'Nothing... Nothing. This seemed like a good idea but...' She shrugged. 'I'm not really feeling it.'

She looked as if she wasn't feeling anything, but Ross knew better. She'd learned to work through any pain by just pretending she didn't feel anything, and the more impassive her face, the more she was struggling.

'What's this for?' He reached out and brushed the model boat with his fingertips. As he did so, he saw that it was full of kindling, and that a box of matches lay on the bench beside her. Laurie was saying goodbye to something... someone.

'He's been gone a long time. Fifteen years ago today.' She turned, looking at him solemnly. 'I've spent almost as much time without him as I had with him.'

'And you thought you might send the boat

out onto the water? As a remembrance for someone you've lost?'

'Yes, it's a model I had at home and… I put it into my case when we went down to London. I don't know whether it's the right thing now.'

'If you make it the right thing, then that's what it is.'

She looked at him thoughtfully. 'It won't make any difference.'

'No, it won't. Sometimes remembering someone and saying whatever you want to them makes a difference to you, though.'

She nodded. Ross wondered whether Laurie was so used to concealing her feelings that she wouldn't be able to break through her impassive mask now, but he knew one thing. She wanted to.

'I'll do you a deal. If you push your boat off from here it'll just float back to the shore. I have a pair of waders and I can take it out far enough to catch the current. You can say what you want to say and maybe that'll float away too.'

She thought for a moment and then nodded. Ross got to his feet, hurrying back to his apartment before Laurie changed her mind.

Laurie had been sitting here for over an hour, waiting for a moment that never seemed to come, when she could get in touch with her feelings and make some sense of them. All she could feel right now, on the anniversary of the death of her older brother, was overwhelming pain and terrible guilt.

Maybe she'd been waiting for Ross, to come out here and make sense of it all for her. That was rather too much to ask of anyone.

He was back before she could make any sense of wanting him here either, putting the waders onto the ground next to the bench and sitting down.

'Who's the boat for, Laurie?'

Good. Questions that were easy to answer.

'My older brother, Tom. He died when I was fifteen.'

'He must have been young.' Ross shook his head, understanding the terrible waste of a life that should have been just beginning.

'He was twenty-one.' Laurie puffed out a sigh and suddenly it became a little easier to talk. 'My father pushed all of us to strive for sporting careers. Tom was going to be the tennis player, but my younger brother Ben was always more talented. My father pushed and pushed and...he pushed Tom too hard.'

'What was he best at? The thing you'd most like to remember him for?'

No one asked that. Tom had been caught in

a cycle of the wrong expectations and failure, and that was what defined his death as well as his life.

'He was kind, and very funny. He used to make me finger puppets when I was little and we'd make our own plays with them. Tom always came out with the best lines.' All the warmth came flooding back at the memory. Along with pain. But it was better than the emptiness that she'd been sitting here with.

'He sounds great.'

'He was really creative and he used to tell the best stories. For my tenth birthday, he made me a book about a dragon who made everyone around him do as he said…we both knew that was really my father. One day he had so much steam coming out of his ears that he exploded. It was…' Laurie choked suddenly, tears spilling down her face.

'Breathe.' Ross murmured the word, putting his arm lightly around her shoulders. 'Breathing helps.'

A great gasp of air *did* help. Somehow the tears were helping as well.

'My father wouldn't see that he wasn't cut out for sport, it wasn't what he wanted to do and he wasn't that good at it either. He just pushed and pushed, telling Tom he was a failure and that our younger brother was better than he was. Tom got hold of steroids from somewhere, in an attempt to make himself acceptable in my father's eyes, and…'

'The usual side effects?'

Laurie nodded. 'Yes, lack of impulse control and aggression. Combined with all the frustration and rejection he was already feeling. He was cycling home and…the lights were against him and he should have given way, but he didn't. He just rode at a lorry, expecting it to stop, and there was no way it could. I was fifteen, and it was then that I decided I had to get out.'

'So…he couldn't save himself, but…maybe he saved you?'

'I don't think he meant to. He was just influenced by the drugs.'

'Maybe. But it sounds as if he loved you very much. What would he say to you now, if he knew that you'd broken free of your father?'

More tears. But somehow the tightness in her chest seemed to be easing now that she was no longer struggling to keep them back.

'I think he'd say that he was happy about that. He'd probably write me a story.'

'Yeah? Then you've got something to thank him for.'

Tom's life seemed less like a catalogue of failure and missed opportunity now. 'Aunt

Suze always used to say that it was all such a waste...'

'She's right, it was a waste of a young life. But what he was, the things he did will never be wasted as long as you remember him for them.'

Laurie wiped her face, picking the boat up from the bench beside her. This wasn't the brave face that she'd put on for her father. It was wanting to say the things she really wanted to, for Tom, and that felt very different.

'Let's do this.'

Ross nodded. 'Yeah. Let's do it.'

He pulled on the waders and they walked down to the water's edge. In the darkness, with Ross standing quietly beside her, Laurie said the things she wanted to say to Tom. Then he put the small boat onto the water and handed her the matches.

Her hands were trembling, and she broke the first two, trying to strike them against the side of the box. But the third flared brightly and she touched it against the kindling in the boat. It started to glow and then caught.

'You want me to take it out now?' Ross spoke quietly.

'Yes, please.' Laurie pressed her fingers against her lips, touching the kiss against the side of the boat, and Ross started to wade out, pushing the boat. The flames were spreading, now, and the fire that she'd carefully built was beginning to lick around the mast.

Suddenly, she had to be a part of this as well. Laurie waded out into the water and he turned, waiting for her.

No comments about how she'd ruin her sandals, or that the water was cold. When she reached him, he pushed the boat towards her and she gingerly took hold of it. They took a few steps more, Ross's hand around her waist steadying her against the pull of the current. This was what she needed to do, and she didn't want to do it alone. She wanted Ross to be with her.

Laurie said one last goodbye and pushed the boat out into the lake. It bobbed for a moment and then the current found it and it started to drift away, a speck of shining flame in the darkness.

She couldn't keep herself from crying again, but she didn't have to. Ross held her tight, the warmth of his body comforting her. Together they watched the boat float away, until finally the flames caught on the infrastructure and the light was extinguished.

Ross, the man who seemed to have an answer for everything, was as lost for words as she was. When she looked up at him, he was staring into the darkness, and Laurie thought she saw the glint of a tear in his eye. A tear for her beloved Tom that moved Laurie more than she could say.

'Thank you, Ross.'

He nodded, taking her hand, and they waded out of the water together. Silent in the darkness and yet so, so close. He watched as she walked awkwardly to the bench, her feet slipping in her wet sandals.

'I can't walk in these…' She sat down, taking them off. The rough ground between here and the cultivated lawn at the back of the house might be a little hard on her feet, but at least she wouldn't slip and fall.

'Want a piggy-back?' Ross was stripping off the waders and pulling on his sneakers.

Probably not the most elegant of ways to leave your brother's tribute, but Tom would have found it funny. And Ross seemed to know that Laurie would have felt awkward about being carried. She stood up on the bench, and climbed onto his back.

'Uh… You're a lot heavier than you look.' Ross didn't seem to be having any trouble carrying her, and was striding towards the house.

'That's because it's all muscle. Where's your knowledge of human anatomy, Ross?' Tom would have found the teasing funny, too.

'Next time I need a lift I'll know who to ask...'

'You think I couldn't?'

He shook his head. 'No. I'm horribly afraid that you could. Keep still, will you?'

Laurie wrapped her arms around his neck, snuggling against him. The warmth of his body penetrated through her wet jeans and his solidity was comforting and...

Maybe she shouldn't be feeling that. But Tom wouldn't have minded, he would have just laughed and told her to go for it. He would have understood the damage that her father had done, how she hadn't been able to consider the thought of a happy family or a relationship because all those things seemed like a prison to her. And maybe he'd understand how her feelings were beginning to change.

But, however much she trusted Ross, however much he trusted her, it still couldn't change anything. He didn't trust the future, and Laurie knew that he wouldn't go any further than a few kisses, which they could pretend hadn't happened.

He reached the patio and let her down gently from his back. She couldn't let him go now, and she caught hold of his hand, feeling his fingers wind around hers.

'Thank you, Ross. That was…everything I wanted it to be.'

He nodded. 'It was an honour to share it with you.'

Still she couldn't leave him. But Ross pulled his hand away from hers. 'You should get inside and get dry. Maybe take a shower to get rid of the Eau de Pondweed…'

'You don't like it?'

'It has a mysterious allure. You may want to check in your pockets for fish, though. Why don't I make some hot chocolate? I'll meet you on the steps.' He gestured towards the spiral staircase that led up to his balcony.

'I've got hot chocolate. And plenty of milk.' She didn't want him to leave her for even a few minutes.

'Your place, then…' His grin made her shiver. Hot chocolate, your place or mine. That wasn't the way Ross did things. An invitation for drinks was just that, and your place or mine was a matter of which was more convenient.

She caught his hand, leading him into the small apartment. The drapes had been drawn all day, the light had hurt her eyes too much to let any of it in, but now she wanted to see the lake. She drew the curtains back, letting in the moonlight that reflected off the water.

He shooed her towards the bathroom, her

jeans leaving a trail of water behind her. When she returned, he'd wiped the floor, plumped the cushions on the sofa, where she'd been sitting all day, and put the coffee cups into the sink. And there were two mugs steaming on the breakfast bar.

'This is nice. Thank you for this evening.' Laurie sat down next to him on the sofa, and he stretched his arm out on the cushions behind her. It was an open invitation for a hug, and she moved closer, taking him up on it.

CHAPTER ELEVEN

ROSS HAD BEEN thinking a lot about this. How right it seemed, and how very wrong he'd been. Laurie had changed. She'd learned how to trust the people around her, and that showing her feelings wasn't such a bad thing. She didn't need him any more, and it was time to let her go.

He waited until the day had run its course, knowing when he'd have an opportunity to find her alone. Laurie was a creature of habit, and she liked to go down to the lake after work and just sit for a while, watching the movement of the water. Maybe she saw something there that he didn't, currents that might shift a boat forward a little or impede its progress. Or maybe she just liked the view.

He said down next to her and she smiled. A *real* smile, open-faced and bright-eyed as if she was genuinely happy. It made Ross happy too, and rendered what he was about to do next all the more difficult.

'I have something for you.' He gave her the envelope he'd been carrying.

'Yes? What's this?' She opened the flap, taking out the sheet of paper and scanning it.

Significant progress...
Positive attitude...
Confident that Dr Sullivan is committed to improving her condition, and that she will continue to improve after she leaves...

'Leaves the clinic?' Laurie picked out the words that Ross had typed then deleted and retyped three times. 'What have I done *now*, Ross?'

'You've done nothing. Why would you think...?'

She waved the paper at him ferociously. 'Because this sounds a lot as if you're giving me the sack.'

Clearly she was in no mind to make this easy for him. 'I'm not giving you the sack. Read the letter, Laurie.'

'Yes, I'm reading it. It says lots of nice things about me, and how I don't need you any more.'

'You don't. You never did.'

'I needed you, Ross. I needed someone to

give me a shake and make me realise what I was doing to myself. And this…' She flipped the letter with her finger. '*This* is how you give someone the sack. You give a really nice reference and then cut them loose. After you *promised* me that I could help these kids.'

Ross didn't recall actually promising anything of the kind. But she was right, he had told her that she could take charge of Adam and Tamara's treatment, and she'd made an excellent job of it. He expected all the staff at the clinic to know that his word was as good as a promise.

'It's the right thing—'

'No! It's *not* the right thing. If you want me to go you should just say so.'

He didn't want her to go. But that was the whole point of this. Somewhere, deep inside, her anger was making him want to reach out and hug her. More than just hug her.

'You're not understanding what I'm doing…'

'No, actually, I don't. Try explaining it to me. Words of one syllable, please.'

Ross took a breath. He'd worked all of this out in his head, and he was sure that he was doing the right thing. Only he'd hoped that Laurie might look at the letter and realise that this was the right thing to do, too, without the need for explanations.

'All right. Simmer down.'

'No, I will *not* simmer down, Ross. This is…too much.' She crumpled the paper in her hand, dropping it at her feet. The wind caught it, and it bounced across the grass, lodging against some stones at the water's edge.

'That's just a copy. I've already sent the original to your consultant.'

'Without telling me? Where do you get off manipulating me, Ross?'

That was exactly his point. It had to stop now.

'Look, Laurie. Three weeks ago I made you an offer it was impossible to refuse. I told you that the clinic wouldn't treat you any more, knowing full well that this place was your last chance.'

'That's right.' She shot him a fierce look.

'I didn't know then that you'd spent your whole childhood being forced into a mould, or that you'd lost your brother. But that's no excuse, I shouldn't have done it.'

Laurie crossed her arms, staring out over the lake and refusing to meet his gaze. 'We've been through that, Ross. I've admitted that I was being unreasonable, and you stopped me from cutting off my nose to spite my face.'

'It doesn't mean that what I did was right.'

There was a sudden flash of warmth in her

eyes. Angry warmth. 'So…what? You're feeling guilty because I got better? Perhaps you should think about taking up another career because doctor doesn't seem to suit you.'

She was deliberately missing the point and the words he'd wanted to say came out in a rush before he could stop them. 'I *care* for you, Laurie. More than I should… I want you to stay, which is what makes it so very wrong of me to compel you to do so.'

'So why on earth didn't you just say so?' The fire was back again. And Laurie's fire could so easily turn to passion.

'Because… If I could offer you more then I'd do it, right here and now. But that's not right for either of us, and you know it. This letter means you're free to go.'

Her eyes widened and she opened her mouth to protest, then closed it again. Laurie knew just as well as he did that a relationship couldn't work between them. There was really nothing more to say.

Standing up and turning his back on her was difficult. And the words she called after him hit him like a knife between his shoulder blades.

'Ross! Don't you walk away…'

He had no choice. This was the right thing to do but he was in imminent danger of taking it all back, just to see Laurie's smile again. When Ross reached the fire escape steps that led up to his apartment, he had the opportunity to turn and glance behind him.

Laurie had walked down to the shore of the lake and was bending to pick up the crumpled letter. That was something, at least. Maybe if she read it again, she'd understand.

A sleepless night brought no answers apart from the ones she didn't want to acknowledge. Three weeks ago, Laurie would have taken the letter and gone, without looking back. Ross couldn't have timed things any worse by giving it to her now, when all she wanted to do was stay.

The morning brought no knock on her door, and she didn't have the heart to knock on his. If this was what Ross really wanted, then she should leave. Laurie left a message for Sam, asking if she was free for lunch, and set to work. She didn't want to think about having to say goodbye to the friends she'd made here, or to Tamara and Adam, but she was going to have to.

Sam tapped on the French doors at lunchtime, looking a little worried. She proffered a couple of herbal teabags, which was a sure sign that she thought something was up.

'Mmm. That looks nice.' She perched herself on one of the stools at the breakfast bar and snagged a slice of tomato from the large mixed salad that Laurie took out of the fridge. 'What's going on?'

'I'm going to leave. Tomorrow, probably.'

'Leave?' Sam's eyes widened in surprise. 'But I thought you were staying for another three weeks.'

'Yeah. I was going to.' Laurie flipped the kettle on.

'So…' Sam puffed out a breath. 'You haven't had an argument with Ross, have you?'

'Has he said anything?' Laurie shouldn't ask, but her curiosity got the better of her.

'No. He actually hasn't said anything to anyone all morning. Something's bugging him.'

'He wrote me a letter.'

Sam stared at her. 'A letter?'

She should just tell Sam she had to go. Hand over her notes on Adam and Tamara and leave it at that. But the nagging hope that somehow there was a way that she could stop what was happening wouldn't let her.

'Help yourself.' Laurie pushed the salad bowl towards Sam. 'I'll show you.'

She fetched the letter, laying it on the counter. Sam took a sip of her tea and picked it up.

'Has this been through the washing machine or something?'

'No, I…um… I screwed it into a ball and threw it.'

'Oh. Feelings running high, then.' Sam smiled, as if that wasn't such a bad thing at all. Then she focussed on the letter, reading it through as she ate.

'I'll agree this sounds like something you'd write when someone's leaving. But isn't this what you wanted, Laurie? Ross has given you what you need to square things with your consultant.'

'He said it meant I was free to go. I'm assuming that's what he wants.'

Sam narrowed her eyes. 'You're sure about that? Let me read the letter again.'

There was no point in trying to eat. Laurie watched miserably while Sam re-read the letter.

'Well, I can't get inside his head.' Sam laid the paper back down and took a swig of her tea. 'But I've known Ross for a while, and… when he decides that something's wrong he just can't let it go. It's admirable actually, but it can be annoying.'

'So…what do you think?'

'Ross didn't want to box you into a corner the way he did. If it's anyone's fault it's mine, because I told him that you weren't following my advice…' Sam turned the corners of her mouth down.

'You were right. I would have done the same. I was being unreasonable and I'm really sorry—'

'That's water under the bridge.' Sam grabbed Laurie's hand, squeezing it. 'I'm only bringing it up because I know that Ross wasn't happy about not giving you the choice, it's against everything he believes in. I don't know, but I think this may be all about that and nothing to do with wanting you to leave.'

'Too much of a gentleman, you mean?'

Sam snorted with laughter. 'Yes. It's not a bad thing, I suppose.'

'No. It's quite a nice thing really.'

There was a lot of sense in what Sam said, but Laurie had been too upset and disappointed to see it before. So afraid of rejection that she'd jumped to that conclusion far too quickly and not looked behind Ross's words.

'What are you going to do?' Sam was looking at her thoughtfully.

'I'm going to make it clear to him that I want to stay. I want to finish what I've started with Adam and Tamara, and I want to continue on here with my own exercise regime.

This place gives me the framework that I need to get better.'

Sam nodded. 'Sounds good to me. If Ross has a problem with that, he'll say so.'

There *was* a problem, one that Laurie hadn't told Sam about. Ross had said he cared for her, and that he'd take things further if only he could. But maybe she could find a way for them both to do that as well.

Seduction. That was the way forward. If it didn't work, she could leave and put it down to experience. But Laurie had thought about this carefully, and it was what she wanted. It was what Ross had said he'd wanted, too.

The only problem was that she'd left the only really nice dress she had at home, along with the high-heeled sandals that went with it. That was a difficulty, but problems were there to be solved. Maybe a less obvious approach would be better anyway. If she made a joke of it, maybe they could laugh their way out of any embarrassment.

She slipped into a pair of thick black leggings, and dark-coloured trainers. A black polo-necked sweater she'd brought, in case the weather turned cold, was ideal and the dark blue woollen hat that she wore for rowing covered her hair.

Laurie slipped out of her apartment, looking up at the balcony. The French doors stood slightly open, as they did most nights, to let fresh air into his bedroom. Further along, a light in the sitting-room window told her where he was. She took the dark blue scarf she'd brought with her and tied it around her face, like a bandana.

Now or never. If she didn't do this now, she'd have to go tomorrow, because now she knew he wanted her, she couldn't take another day of wanting him without touching him. Laurie crept silently up the wrought-iron stairs to the balcony, slipping in through the French windows like a shadow.

The bedroom was deserted, as she'd expected. It had a masculine feel about it, with oatmeal-coloured walls and heavy oak furniture. In one corner, a solid free-standing mirror, the kind you saw in gentlemen's outfitters, and a mass of framed pictures and photographs on the wall. It was somehow cosy and…

It had a bed. That was the only thing that Laurie was really interested in. Maybe she'd find out whether the mattress was as soft as it looked, if things went her way this evening.

She heard footsteps in the hallway. She hadn't thought she'd made any noise and was wondering how best to attract Ross's attention, but it seemed he knew she was here. When he reached the open doorway, she saw his smile, and a stab of desire made her legs tremble.

'What do you want?'

He knew exactly what she wanted. The look on his face told Laurie that. But Ross would always test her, always make her say it. His gaze was fixed on her face and she pulled the bandana down. That had probably been a bad idea because she needed him to see her face and know that she was serious about this. Resolute.

'You told me that I was free to do as I wanted now. I know you believe that we don't have any future together and I respect that. But this is what I want, Ross. To be with you tonight.'

'To talk?' He took one step forward. Ross knew darned well that they'd done quite enough talking.

'No.' She flipped her finger towards the bed. 'I want you right there.'

Suddenly he grinned. That taste of mischief that made her heart thump in her chest and set her thinking about all the things that she and Ross could do together. Then he pulled his polo shirt over his head, letting it drop onto the carpet.

Beautiful. Ross had the kind of body that

was made for pleasure, and a great deal of appreciation. She stepped forward, finding his arms, and then he kissed her.

It was like everything else between them. Two strong characters fighting for dominance, but both wanting the same thing. He left her in no doubt about what he wanted. When she caught her breath, pulling him closer, he smiled down at her and then kissed her again. He was going to make this night perfect.

Ross had been sitting in the pool of light around a lamp. Plenty of reading matter on the sofa beside him, along with the remote for the TV, but he couldn't set his mind to any of it. He hadn't seen Laurie for twenty-four hours, and it already felt as if she'd gone.

He heard a sound. The slight creak as the French windows next door opened and a corresponding one again as they closed. That wasn't the breeze. Someone was there, and there was only one person it could be.

He tried to walk slowly to the bedroom. Tried not to jump to conclusions about her presence here, but when he saw her there was only one conclusion. Laurie's sense of humour might be a little wry, but it corresponded with his own. He couldn't help smiling, because he got the joke. A thief in the night, taking what neither of them could commit to during the day.

And she wanted him. As much maybe as he wanted her. If her words hadn't made her purpose here indisputable, then her kiss would have convinced him. Taking everything he wanted to give her, and demanding more.

'You're sure about this…' He couldn't stop himself from asking. 'One night?'

'What makes you think I'm not? Although if you're really good it could be two or three.' She pushed him against the wall, pressing her hips against his and running her hand across his chest. Sheer desire almost made him fall to his knees.

'You want it all your own way, do you?'

Mischief lit in her beautiful eyes. Her hand moved down, unbuttoning the waist of his chinos. 'Try me. Maybe you'll like doing as you're told for once.'

Ross was sure that he would. Less sure that it was what Laurie wanted. They'd always confronted each other, and now that seemed like a complicated, drawn-out foreplay that would shape the night ahead.

'Maybe *you'll* like doing as you're told. You should try that.'

She kissed him, her lips hard and searching

on his. 'If you want it, you're going to have to take it.'

Of course he was. Neither of them would have it any other way. She was strong, but his bulk was a match for her. He lifted her off her feet and carried her over to the mirror. Turning her as he set her down again, so that her back was pressed against his chest.

'Watch.'

'You are *such* a bad man. That's a nice surprise.'

Her obvious enjoyment gave him purpose. Pinning her against him, he removed the scarf around her neck with his free hand. Then pulled her sweater over her head, cupping her breast with one hand, holding her against him with the other. Laurie wriggled a bit, but made no effort to get free. The movement was just a little sweet friction, and looking over her shoulder into the mirror he could see that she liked that as much as he did.

'That feels nice.' She smiled at him in the mirror. 'Not nice enough…'

Ross unhooked her bra, letting it slip over her shoulders. 'Better?'

'Much…' She only just got the word out before his fingers reached her breast and she groaned.

He kissed her neck, his fingers exploring

the way she wanted to be aroused. Keeping her gaze locked in his in the mirror, watching carefully for every emotion.

Ross told her everything, whispering in her ear. There would be no mistake about how much he wanted her, and no mistake about how beautiful she was. Flaming hair and a body that was so strong and yet so soft. When she reached behind her, her fingers searching for the zip of his jeans, he gasped. Seeing his own face and hers, their gazes locked together in binding passion, and feeling what she was doing to him was taking him way beyond anything he'd thought that sex might be able to offer them both.

Suddenly she turned in his arms, stretching up to kiss him. 'You don't get this all your own way, Ross. However much I might like it.'

Laurie backed him towards the bed, and he sat down suddenly when he felt the backs of his legs touch the mattress. He reached for her, but she batted his hands away, slipping her trainers off along with her leggings. Ross followed suit, sliding out of his chinos and shoes. Waiting…

She got up onto the bed, crouching over him, her eyes flickering with the fire that he loved so very much. Laurie was in control now, and the feeling of where that might take him was all-consuming and more delicious than he could ever have imagined.

This was…insanely wonderful. Crazily passionate and yet full of the trust they'd built up over the last few weeks. He was watching her every move, shifting back on the bed when she flipped her finger towards the pillows. When she moved his searching hands away from her body, he resisted just enough to allow her to push against him, but not enough to make any difference.

There was so much to admire about his body. When she did so with her tongue, running it across his chest and teasing his nipples, he groaned. This was payback time for all the delicious things he'd done to her. The way he'd held her in front of the mirror and made her watch, which made it all even more delicious because she could see the gentle mischief in his eyes.

'You're killing me, Laurie.' He choked out the words as her fingers gently worked their way downwards. Slowly, because she liked the response it prompted in him so much.

'You want me to stop?' She allowed her hand to brush lightly against his erection.

'No. I just want you to…' He groaned, his

head snapping back as she went back again, this time with a more substantial caress.

'That?'

'Yeah. That.'

This was so much fun. Laurie had always reckoned that there were guys who were great friends and other guys who were great in bed. Ross was both, and they were just the same now as they always were. Pushing each other, challenging each other for control. Working it out, because he had the same sense of humour as she did, and he wasn't afraid to use it.

'Are you ready for me?' She grinned down at him.

'Are you quite mad? What do you think?'

'I think…not quite.' She bent down, kissing the overwhelming evidence that he *was* ready, hearing the sharp hiss of breath escaping his lungs.

'Uh… Yeah, you're right. Now I'm definitely ready.' He caught her hand as she slid away from him. 'Where are you going now?'

'Condoms. In my pocket.' Her leggings were…somewhere. Breaking away from him to find them was such a waste of those moments when she couldn't touch him. But she knew that it was important to Ross that the one in a thousand chance became no chance at all. He had to be free of those worries.

He reached out, flipping open the drawer of the cabinet beside the bed. 'There are some in there.'

Finding them was the ultimate pleasure, because Ross's hands on her body made her fight to keep from forgetting about the contents of the drawer. Tearing the packet open was an exercise in trying to focus while he caressed her breasts.

'Stop that, Ross. You know how many people rip holes in condoms in just this situation?' She gritted her teeth, trying to think about the article she'd read about that recently, and failing miserably.

'I couldn't give you an exact figure right now.'

He took the condom from her shaking fingers, and she watched as he rolled it into place. As she straddled him, lowering herself slowly down to take him inside her, his gaze held hers captive.

Two deep sighs, hers and his, which might have been one because they were simultaneous. When she twisted her hips, the feeling made her cry out and a groan escaped his lips. And when she bent to kiss him, he was ready and waiting with kisses of his own.

They were together. No more vying for control, each trying to please the other. Everything was shared, every pleasure she felt found its way onto his lips as well. She melted into his arms and he whispered her name, shifting her gently onto her back. When he slid inside her again, the idea that they were just having sex exploded into smithereens. This was making love.

He was so tender, so exquisitely passionate. Their bodies moved together in the same rhythm, making the very most of the intimate connection they shared. It was no longer a matter of holding back, making this last, but of relishing the feeling that was growing inside her. She could do nothing but allow him to take her, knowing that he too was in her thrall.

When she came, it was a long fall into mindless pleasure. She knew she was pulling him with her, and as aftershocks tingled through her body, his hardened suddenly. He let out a cry, and she held onto him, knowing that he needed her touch as much as she had needed his.

'That was...' What they'd done defied description.

'Crazy?' He grinned down at her, lifting his weight and rolling onto his side to hold her close.

'Complete madness.' She kissed him. If this

was madness then every day could be this insane as far as Laurie was concerned.

‘It was beautiful.’ He murmured the words, tenderness in his face.

‘Yes. Beautiful is the word I was searching for.’

CHAPTER TWELVE

THEY'D DOZED FOR a long time, happy to just be in each other's arms. Then Laurie felt Ross shift against her as he leaned around to kiss her.

'Are you really going to leave at dawn?' His finger caressed her shoulder.

'Yes.' If what they had together was going to survive, it needed to be separate. Away from the limitations that practicality put on their relationship. 'I'll see you later, though? At the clinic?'

Ross grinned. 'So you're not going very far.'

'Not so far that I can't come back again, to-morrow night. Or be at the clinic during the day. If that's okay with you.'

He shot her a reproachful look. 'I always wanted you to stay. Are you seriously in any doubt about that?'

'If I had been, I probably wouldn't have crept up the stairs onto your balcony. I'd have knocked on your front door in order to preserve deniability.'

He chuckled quietly. 'I prefer the balcony.' He rolled onto his back, putting his hands behind his head.

'Me too. Maybe I can try swarming up it dressed as a pirate. With a cutlass between my teeth.'

'Absolutely not. That's *my* fantasy, so you can keep your hands off it.'

'Your fantasy? Really? You mean finding me up here in one of those floaty nightgowns, and popping the buttons with the tip of your sword? I'd have to keep pretty still...'

'I'd anchor you to the spot with my dangerous gaze.' He chuckled. 'And then...' He leaned over, whispering into her ear, and Laurie started to shiver from the exquisite pictures he was planting in her imagination.

'Stop!' Finally she called a halt to it. 'Stop it, Ross. You're not allowed to say that to me unless you're willing to come up with the goods. Straight away.'

'I'm more than happy to do that.' He grinned at her.

'In that case...' She reached across him, hooking another condom out of the drawer and pressing it into his hand. 'I have a few fantasies of my own you might like. Only you don't get to hear them until you give me a bit of encouragement.'

He chuckled softly then tore the packet open. 'I'll give you all the encouragement you want...'

Ross was exhausted. The kind of exhaustion that came from staying awake half the night, talking and making love, and then being woken at four o'clock for one of the best good mornings he'd ever had. *The* best, actually.

He'd caught Laurie yawning as she'd got back into her clothes and had called after her as she'd slipped through the French doors. She'd nodded, agreeing that there was still time to get some sleep before they were due at work at nine.

Laurie had the best poker face he'd ever seen. He already knew that, but it was still a little unsettling. She greeted him with her usual smile, nothing in her face reflecting what they'd been doing together last night. He wondered if she'd somehow managed to forget, and decided that wasn't possible.

She knocked on his open office door at eleven, and he looked up and beckoned her in. Laurie closed the door behind her, which was the generally accepted signal that he was in conference with someone and not available.

Maybe now her impressive composure would crack.

'I've got an idea. There's a games convention at a hotel thirty miles from here, and I want to take Adam. He really wants to go.'

'Right. Well, I'm sure it would be a nice day out for him.' Ross wondered how that was going to help Adam's foot.

'It's not just that, Ross. Adam's our model patient, you know that. He does all his exercises in the gym, he's made friends, he's eaten well and slept when he's supposed to.'

'But he's not getting out of the wheelchair, is he?' Ross had noticed that Adam spent most of his free time playing video games.

'No, he isn't. He isn't confident about his recovery, and it's as if he's putting off the bad news. That he'll get better and still not be able to run again.'

'And a games convention's going to solve that?' If Laurie thought it would then Ross was willing to give it a go.

'I want to try. I gave Ann a call and she thinks it's a really good idea, if we don't mind taking him. Will you come?'

'Okay. I can get Mum to pop in and cover for me and take a day out.'

'Thanks, Ross. I really think this might be a turning point for him.'

Ross leaned back in his chair. 'So how long are you going to be able to keep this up, then?'

She grinned at him suddenly, her cheeks flushing. The kind of look you gave a guy when you'd just spent the night with him, and Ross was surprised at how much it meant to him.

'Stop! I thought I was doing so well!'

'You were. *I'd* never have known what you were up to last night, and I was there. It's actually quite unnerving. I was beginning to wonder if you were suffering from a memory lapse.'

'That's my thing. Don't show what you're thinking. One of the things I learned from my father.'

It was the first time that Laurie had ever said it. Maybe that was the most solid piece of evidence that last night *had* happened. She was finally breaking out of the isolation that her troubled childhood had imposed on her life.

'It's not the way you have to be, Laurie. You can decide for yourself.'

She nodded. 'That's still under consideration. But it doesn't do any harm to keep this quiet. No one here needs to know that I slept with the boss, do they?'

'No, they don't. As long as *you* remember it…' Ross's words were only half in jest. He knew that their relationship couldn't last but he didn't want it to be swallowed up in her single-minded determination. Lost for ever behind her impassive eyes.

'I remember.' She laughed suddenly, scrunching a loose piece of paper from her pad into a tight ball and throwing at him. Ross batted it away, smiling.

'How was your hip this morning?'

'Official answer?'

He nodded. 'If you like. Then I'll take the real one.'

'The official answer is that it's improving steadily. The real one is that I noticed you were careful last night, and…you were perfect. It doesn't hurt at all this morning.' The red of her cheeks deepened slightly. 'You were perfect in every other way as well.'

'You make me *want* to be perfect. It's what you deserve.'

He wasn't perfect, not by a very long way. He couldn't give Laurie a home or a family, because his home was the clinic, and that was the only family he'd ever have. It was a good life, but Laurie had a whole world out there and a whole life of her own. But that didn't mean they couldn't take a little time out of their lives for each other and move on a little richer for it.

'Would you like to come to me tonight?' She

gave him an impish grin. 'Just so that I don't start to feel I'm stalking you.'

'I'll be there.'

Laurie nodded. There was a moment of shared warmth when her gaze caught his, and then she stood. No kiss but, then, it was a little inappropriate in this setting. Here they were just temporary colleagues, and they'd closeted themselves in his office to talk about their patients.

But tonight… When the sun began to go down, Ross took the bottle of champagne from the refrigerator, putting it into a shopping bag in case anyone should see him. But he was alone in the quiet warmth of the evening as he hurried down the steps from the balcony, tapping on the French doors of Laurie's apartment. She was waiting for him, unlatching the door and beckoning him in, and he stepped inside and took her into his arms.

'You're sure about this.' Ross looked around the foyer of the hotel.

'Positive. Ann's all for it.'

'Yeah, but…did she know about the costumes?'

'Of course she does. Everyone wears costumes to video game events.'

'I wasn't expecting them to be quite so revealing, though.' Ross nodded towards a young woman dressed up as some kind of warrior with a sword. Her body armour could only be described as skimpy.

'Oh! She's my avatar!'

'Really? You wander around on the screen dressed like that, do you?' He couldn't help grinning.

'Excuse me. I do *not* wander, I stalk. Anyway, she's wearing body paint.' Laurie narrowed her eyes. 'Let's hope it's non-allergenic or we'll be picking her up off the floor.'

'But Ann does know what *kind* of costumes….'

'She knows. She's taken Adam to these things before. He's sixteen.' She pursed her lips. 'You really did have a sheltered childhood, didn't you?'

'Yeah. Suppose I did.' Ross looked over to where Adam was sitting in his wheelchair, perusing the different programmes for the event. He seemed to be taking it all in his stride and had accepted a leaflet from the woman warrior without giving her a second glance.

He followed Laurie over to the stand, watching as she took the standard programme out of Adam's hands and picked up the thicker collector's copy, passing a note from her purse over to the young man behind the counter.

'These are the ones I want to go to.' Adam flipped carefully through the pages of the programme.

'Okay.' Laurie looked over his shoulder. 'Yes, we have to go to that one, it's our game. Should we mark the ones you want?'

'No!' Adam looked at her as if she'd suggested defacing the Mona Lisa. 'If you have the collector's copy of the programme, the idea is that you get autographs from people on the pages. See, the paper's different, for signing.'

'Seems I've got a bit to learn. Shall we take one of those free ones for marking where we want to go, then?'

Adam nodded. 'Yes, that's a good idea. We should have one each.'

'Great plan. I definitely think Ross could do with one, he's got no idea what's going on.' She shot Ross a smile, as if expecting him to protest.

'You're right. Not a clue.' But he trusted Laurie. If she thought that this was going to work, he'd give it a shot. If it didn't work then at least it was a nice day out for Adam.

The stack of free programmes was at the end of the counter and Laurie waited a moment to see whether Adam would reach for them, before pushing the wheelchair a little closer. It was a good try, and if Ross knew Laurie she'd have a few more up her sleeve.

He pushed the wheelchair and Laurie walked by the side of it. They visited stands, got autographs and Adam chatted to people in costumes about strange other worlds. The other visitors to the event were all good-humoured, if sometimes rather garishly dressed, and the enormous hall meant that the crowd wasn't too densely packed.

'This is so great. The one that Mum and I went to in London was really crowded and we could hardly see anything. Here you can get to the stalls and see stuff.'

'You'd see a bit more if you stood up.' Laurie floated the idea.

'No.' Adam shook his head quickly. 'It's fine, I can see. Thanks for bringing me.'

'I'm really enjoying myself. Ooh, look!' Laurie pointed to a large circular stand at the centre of the hall. 'There's our game. We have to go there.'

'Yeah. Look, there's your avatar.' Adam grinned. 'It would be really cool to get her signature, along with one from mine.'

Ross wheeled the chair over to the stand. Six steep steps led up to the central space where there was a landscape of trees with a backdrop showing an ancient castle, with various people in costumes engaged in swordfights. The woman he'd seen in the armour and body paint seemed to be making short work of her rather lumbering opponent.

'Just be a minute.' Laurie left Ross and Adam watching the fights, disappearing around the side of the stand. She reappeared again, smiling.

'What?' Ross murmured to her.

'No ramps. That means that Adam's going to have to walk up the steps. I know he can do it…' She turned the corners of her mouth down. 'Although I'll still be giving the organisers a piece of my mind. They should have made everything wheelchair accessible.'

'Yeah, I'll join you. Although we don't need to go up there, do we?' Adam had already collected the freebies that were available on other stalls from costumed characters who were wandering around the sides of the stall, and tucked them carefully into the backpack he'd brought.

'Photographs. I spotted them taking photographs up there a while ago. I think they're doing it between fights.'

'Has it occurred to you that they'll probably see the wheelchair and come down here? No one's going to let a kid in a wheelchair miss out.'

Laurie frowned. 'I'll think of something.'

When the fights finished, and people started to go up the steps to the podium, she left Adam's side, walking straight up to her avatar and speaking to her. The woman listened and nodded, then turned to Adam and waved. But she didn't come down the steps. Then Laurie re-joined them.

'They can't come down. Something to do with having their photos taken with the proper backdrops. We'll have to go up to them.'

Adam looked at the steps speculatively. If this didn't work, Ross wasn't sure what would.

'I'll help you, Adam. It'll be just like the way you do it in the gym.'

'I don't know...' Adam was looking up at the podium.

Ross felt a tap on his shoulder and turned to see a man dressed as an intergalactic warrior. 'Excuse me? I'll go and get my mates, and if the lad wants to go up there, we'll carry him. Bloody outrageous they don't have a ramp.'

'Thank you.' Ross ushered the man away from Adam so he couldn't hear the conversation. 'Thing is, this is his favourite video game and walking up there himself would mean a lot to him...'

He assured the man that his offer was much appreciated but that they didn't need any help, and agreed that they should complain that there was no ramp for wheelchairs. When he turned back towards the stall, he saw Laurie bending down to release the brakes on the wheelchair. She gave him a smile that clearly concealed disappointment.

'Let's go for some lunch, shall we?'

She was a little subdued as she filled the cafeteria tray with sandwiches and drinks, then led the way out into a large open-air seating area. Laurie found a table and sat down. Adam was leafing through his catalogue, the disappointment over the photos seemingly forgotten.

'Here's the thing, Adam.' Laurie gently caught his attention. 'I know exactly what you can and can't do. I know that you need a wheelchair to come here, because it's too much for you to walk around the exhibition. But I also know that you could make those steps, if you wanted to.'

Adam shrugged. 'It's okay. No big deal.'

'Well, it's a big deal to me, because I want to see you get better. I know that you wanted to go up and have your photo taken.'

Laurie had decided to confront Adam. She'd worked hard to make a relationship with the boy, and he trusted her. If she thought this was the right time, then it was.

'Suppose I fall.'

'You won't. Ross and I won't let you.'

'My foot…it isn't better yet.'

'No, it isn't, that's going to take a while. But you can do this, we've climbed steps in the gym together.'

Adam sat silently, shaking his head.

'I think I know why you won't.' Ross saw a glint of determination in Laurie's eye, which told him she wasn't giving up now.

'No, you really don't.' The boy reached for his drink, opening it and putting one of the straws from the tray into the bottle.

'I know how hard sport can be sometimes. But one thing I've learned is that you can't not try things because you might fail. If you can't run again, that's going to be difficult to deal with. But if you don't do the things you *can* do, it'll be even worse.'

Ross felt a tickle of embarrassment at the back of his neck. Was Laurie talking about him, too? He dismissed the thought. She knew how he felt and she accepted it.

'Let me tell you something. I came close to giving up at one point and ruining all my chances of ever getting back into competition rowing. But there's one thing I know for sure.'

The chatter of the seating area suddenly receded into the background. If Laurie didn't have Adam's attention, she had Ross's. She was using her own hopes and fears to reach the boy, and that took nerve and commitment.

'What?'

Laurie smiled, leaning towards Adam. 'I know that whatever I can and can't do in the future, I'll have tried for my dreams. If I fail, that's just as much a badge of courage as if I succeed.'

Ross swallowed down the lump in his throat. Maybe if someone had said something like that to him during the dark days after Alice had left, he might have felt a little better. Not great, he still would have felt the failure keenly. But somehow justified in having allowed himself to hope.

'I don't know what I'll do if I can't get back to running. I'm not much good at anything else.'

'You'll find something. I know a winner when I see one.' Laurie gave him a smile.

'Okay. We'll give it a go.'

'Great. Then you can sign *my* programme, eh?'

CHAPTER THIRTEEN

LAURIE HAD WHEELED Adam back to the podium, and he'd got unsteadily to his feet. Then something had happened that she clearly hadn't planned for. The woman playing her avatar strode over to the edge of the stage and held her sword aloft in a salute. The other characters had seen what she was doing and followed her lead.

'I've got to do it now.' Adam's brow creased.

'You've already done it, mate.' Ross grinned at him and the boy's back straightened a little.

Slowly, carefully they walked up the steps. Adam was holding onto his arm but he didn't need the support. Just the confidence. And his attention was all on the top of the steps, where the group of costumed performers was waiting for him.

As he reached the top, the woman knelt, holding the hilt of her sword out towards

Adam. It was a little over-theatrical, but Adam flushed red with pleasure, looking up at Ross.

'I'd take it if she offered it to me,' Ross murmured to him.

'Wait!' Laurie was ahead of them, her phone in her hand, and when she rapped out the word the performers froze into warlike poses, used to people wanting photographs. It was perfect. Adam smiled, and Laurie took as many photographs as she could.

He took the sword. Leaning on Ross's arm, Adam was led around to the other side of the podium, which was a reconstruction of a scene inside a castle. Ross led him to the elaborate-looking throne and sat him down.

Then more photographs. Laurie was recording this all as the performers gathered around the throne, taking up different poses, all obviously rehearsed. Adam was grinning now.

As each of the performers took their turn to sign Adam's programme, Ross held out his hand to Laurie to take her phone. 'You go. He'll want a few of you both with your avatars.'

Laurie hesitated, and then nodded. 'He's having such a good time. I'm going to cry in a minute if I'm not careful...'

This meant so much to her. And Ross was so proud of her.

'I might join you. If you're not careful.'

She chuckled, wiping her hand vigorously across her face. 'Don't you dare. I'm relying on you to help me keep it all together.'

The performers seemed in no hurry and everyone else was standing back to give Adam more than his allotted time for photographs. And the customary bravado of a sixteen-year-old was looking as if it was going to crack at any moment.

'There are other people...' Adam gave the sword back to the woman warrior. She bent and kissed him on the cheek and Ross saw Adam's ears redden furiously.

'You have all the photos you want?' Her soft, Newcastle accent sounded slightly at odds with her warlike appearance.

'Yes. Thank you.' Adam watched her go, and then turned to Laurie. 'I want to go back now.'

'You're sure? Isn't there a bit more for us to see?'

'I've done everything I wanted to do. More...' Adam looked around the hall from his vantage point, perched on the throne.

'Okay. Just one more photo. Shift up a bit.' Laurie sat down on the wide seat, next to Adam, holding out her phone for a selfie. 'Smile, Adam. This is what winning feels like.'

* * *

'Who knew those conventions were so hard on the feet?' Laurie flopped down onto Ross's bed.

'Foot rub?'

'Oh, Ross. You say the nicest things. I don't suppose you could take your clothes off first, could you?'

He chuckled. 'No, I don't suppose I could. One thing at a time.'

'Really? I can do two things at once, I've been devouring you with my lustful gaze all day.'

'Have you?' Ross obviously liked the idea. 'I wish you'd mentioned that. I thought you were a hundred percent focussed on getting Adam out of that wheelchair. You did a fine job of it, by the way.'

Laurie smiled at the memory. 'It was so good of the people on that stand, wasn't it? All the sword-raising and the pictures.'

'It was great. And I was so proud of you. You have a real talent for inspiring these kids, you know.'

'I was thinking, I'd love to be able to do more of that kind of thing. Working at the emergency GP centre in London is great, and it fits in well with my schedules, but I don't get to follow through on patients the way I have here.'

'Isn't that the problem, though?' Ross sat down on the bed, propping one of her feet up on his leg. 'Can you fit that kind of long-term care around your rowing schedule?'

He started to massage her foot and Laurie sighed. 'That's so nice. You have wonderful fingers, Ross. And, no, I'm not sure that kind of job would be possible during the rowing season. But I won't be competing for ever.'

Maybe she was crazy to think like this. To wonder if there was a place for her here with Ross, doing a job that she loved. To think that he even wanted her to stay, he was so sure that nothing could ever change, and that a new relationship would end as badly as his last.

'You're competing now. You'll have plenty of time when you retire and that might not be for another few years.'

'Yes. I guess so. I should just make the most of it while I can.'

'We both should. Every night and every day.' He laid her foot back down on the bed, shifting forward to kiss her.

If she could just make him believe that she would be happy without a family. But how could she do that when she didn't even know whether it was true? Things had changed so much, in such a short time, and she needed time to catch up. Maybe Ross was right, and letting go was the only way to save them both from pain.

'Every single night? Sure you can keep up the pace?' she teased him.

'Watch me. Sure *you* can?'

'I can only give it my best shot.' She pulled him close, feeling his weight pin her down on the bed. This was the way it was with her and Ross—the power of their lovemaking could chase away everything but the here and now. And he was right here, right now.

Ross watched as Tamara walked across the gravel drive from the entrance to the clinic. Her gait was so much better now that her prosthetic had been refitted, and she was gaining confidence with every day that passed. She was chatting to Laurie, who waved when she saw him sitting by himself on the cast-iron seat that was placed amongst the shrubbery at the front of the building. For all the world as if she wasn't expecting to see him there, and as if her and Tamara's arrival wasn't perfectly timed.

'Nice day.' Laurie grinned at him, plumping herself down on the seat.

'Yeah. I think it's going to be hotter today than yesterday.'

'I'd say you're right.'

That was probably enough said about the weather. Tamara had lowered herself down between them, and she might begin to suspect that something was up if they went into any more detail. Laurie had planned this so carefully for Tamara, and Ross was looking forward to it as much as she was.

The sound of an engine caught Tamara's attention. Well timed. Ross looked towards the entrance to the clinic's grounds and saw a minibus making its way towards them. In contrast to the vehicle's rather battered appearance, the trailer behind it carried three gleaming hulls.

Laurie was watching Tamara's face, as the minibus drew to a halt in front of them. A man got out, stretching his legs, and two women followed. The side doors of the bus opened, and three more men jumped down onto the gravel.

'They must be lost,' Tamara remarked, and Laurie shrugged. One of the men had detached himself from the group and was jogging towards them.

But Tamara couldn't take her eyes off the boats. It was obvious they were a very different kind of craft from the clinic's, and that their light frames and graceful curves were state-of-the-art water-going technology.

'Hi.' The man stopped in front of them. 'I'm looking for Tamara.'

Now *he* had all of Tamara's attention, and she was staring at him open-mouthed. Laurie nudged her, and she let out a breath.

'I'm Tamara.'

'Hey, there. My name's Grant Levelle. We heard you might be interested in coming rowing with us.'

'Yes! Please…' Tamara was on her feet before Ross could hold out his hand to help her.

'Great. Would you like to come and meet the others?' Grant was grinning from ear to ear. Tamara nodded, and he gave Laurie a nod before starting to amble with her at a slow pace towards the minibus.

'When's he going to tell her?' Ross was watching as the group crowded around Tamara, each one shaking her hand as they were introduced.

'Probably…right about now…' She smiled as Grant bent down, pulling up the leg of his tracksuit trousers to reveal his own prosthetic.

Tamara was staring up at him, her eyes shining. Grant took her arm, guiding her out of the way as the rest of the group started to loosen the straps that fixed one of the boats securely to the trailer. He was obviously explaining everything that was happening, and Tamara was hanging on every word.

Laurie turned to him. 'Did you see her face?'

'Yeah. I think you've just made that young lady's day. Probably her whole year.' It was so nice to see Laurie's obvious glee. 'Why don't you go over?'

'I don't want to crowd her. This is her treat.' Laurie was watching the team just as intently as Tamara was as they unfastened the boats from the trailer. This was her life. Her teammates. She'd left them behind to come here, and Ross could see in her eyes how much she'd missed them.

He got to his feet. 'I should welcome them. And let them know where the sandwiches and drinks are.'

'Ah, yes. They'll definitely want to know about sandwiches.' Laurie jumped to her feet, leading him over to the group.

He welcomed each one of them, thanking them for coming and shaking their hands. Laurie hugged both of the women, exchanging jokes with the men and laughing at their suggestions that she'd been taking it easy for the last few weeks and they'd be seeing later how out of shape she was.

The feeling tugged at him like a long-lost

memory. The one kid at school who wasn't part of a group because he lived too far from everyone else. He wasn't a part of this either.

Ross stuffed his hands into his pockets, making an excuse about having to go and see how things were going in the kitchen, and walked away. Laurie and Grant would look after Tamara, and he had other things to do.

Sam was standing inside the main doors of the clinic with a group of patients and staff, all watching what was going on. When she saw him, she fell into step beside him.

'She's in her element, isn't she?'

'Yes. Did you see Tamara's face when Grant showed her his prosthetic?' Ross would treasure that look. The moment that a teenager's future seemed to open up before her eyes.

'Yes, I did. Makes it all worthwhile…' Sam looked up at him thoughtfully. 'Actually, I was referring to Laurie.'

Something cold wound its way around Ross's heart. Sam was right, Laurie's face had lit up in just the same way as Tamara's had when she greeted her teammates. It was a stark reminder that her life wasn't here, with him.

'Yeah. It's a good day for Laurie as well.'

It was good to see everyone again, and to be around the everyday activity of people who took rowing seriously, the unloading of the boats from the trailer and setting them into the water. It was a temptation too. On a nice day like this, she wanted to stretch her shoulders and feel the pull of the oars. But Laurie contented herself with helping Grant make the adjustments needed to one of the sliding seats in the three-person scull, so that Tamara could give it a try.

'Who is that guy, and what's he done with Laurie Sullivan?' Grant joined her on the grass, watching as Ross double-checked Tamara's seat, talking to her and making sure that her position wouldn't put her leg under any strain that she wasn't ready for yet.

'He hasn't done anything with me.' Well… that wasn't entirely true. She and Ross had done a great deal with each other, but that wasn't what Grant meant.

'Someone has. The physio?' Grant nodded towards Sam, who was spending her lunch break making sure that anyone who wanted to come out on the grass and watch could do so.

'No. I made my own rule and I'm sticking to it. No rowing for another couple of weeks.'

'We can't tempt you?' Grant grinned.

'No, you can't. Don't even try. I need to get this hip properly sorted. Then I'll be back.'

'Fair enough.' Grant leaned back on his elbows. 'So you've taken to talent scouting in the meantime?'

Laurie rolled her eyes. 'No. Tamara's not committed to rowing, it's fun for her and something that she can do at the moment. I know that you know the value of that.'

Grant had made the same journey as Tamara was making, and he'd made his choice of sport. Laurie knew he was committed to helping others do the same if he could, and that was why she'd called him. The team was on its way down from Scotland and Grant had persuaded a few of them to stop off for the day with some of the practice boats.

'I know the value of it. I just never thought I'd hear *you* say it.' Grant's voice became a pitch higher in a bad impression of Laurie's. '"*Rowing's a bit of fun. I'm not going on the water until I'm fully fit.*"'

'Well, that's a different side of me you haven't seen before, isn't it? I'm a doctor too...'

Grant nodded, appearing convinced. Laurie wasn't sure she shared the sentiment. She did feel different. She still wanted the water, the way she always had, but there were other things as well. Things that crowded into the box that she usually kept for rowing.

Maybe she was losing her edge. Maybe her father had been right, and too many other things in her life would blunt her resolve and damage her concentration. Even now, she was watching Ross, and not the boats that bobbed on the water.

'You've taken time out before.'

Grant nodded. 'You know I have.'

'Was it difficult? Getting back?' Laurie had convinced herself that this was just a delicious holiday. One full of sunshine, and this peaceful, optimistic place that Ross had built. And Ross himself, of course. She'd adroitly sidestepped the issue of getting back into competitive rowing again, because if she ever dreamed she'd lose that, she couldn't enjoy this.

'Nah. I came back better. Stronger, because I knew exactly what I wanted.'

'I think I will too.'

She obviously hadn't said that with enough conviction, because Grant raised an eyebrow. 'You're sure about that? Your hip *is* improving, isn't it? Not thinking of retiring?'

Laurie chuckled. 'Not while you're still out there for me to beat.'

'In your dreams.'

Ross had finished talking to Tamara and was strolling towards them. He sat down on the grass next to Laurie.

'Nice place you have here.' Grant smiled across at him. 'Good stretch of water.'

'You're always welcome to stop by if you're in the area. If you give me a call we'll find somewhere for you to sleep if you want to stay overnight.' Ross glanced at Laurie. Maybe that was an invitation particularly aimed at her.

'Thanks.' Grant answered before she could. 'Is Tamara ready?'

Ross nodded. 'Ready enough to explode if she doesn't get to go out soon.'

'Great.' Grant got to his feet, rubbing his hands together. 'Let's get her started, then.'

They watched as Tamara walked a few unsteady steps across the grass to meet Grant. He took her hand, tucking it into the crook of his arm and instead of glowering as she usually did when she needed help, Tamara grinned up at him, talking excitedly.

'Grant's made a friend for life.' Ross stated the obvious.

'Yeah. Grant's very committed to helping youngsters and he's so good with them.'

'It's just what she needed. Someone who can show her that she can do anything she wants. We can tell her that...' He turned to her suddenly. 'You were the one who helped her to really see it, though.'

'Just doing my job.'

'No, you weren't. You were doing far more than your job, Laurie.'

'I've been thinking about what we were talking about the other night. You know, keeping on doing this kind of work.'

'Yeah?' Ross flopped down onto his back, staring up at the sky. 'Come to any conclusions?'

'Yes, I have. You're right, I can't be a proper mentor just yet, but I can start setting up a framework. Something that I can develop, with the aim of spending all my time on it later.'

'That would work. Something like a small charity, with lots of room to grow.'

'Yes, exactly. It would be a network, for teenagers. Maybe start with a website where they can find information about good trainers and good medical care. What they want would be the most important thing, not what other people want for them. We'd be entirely without any expectations of what the right answer for them might be.'

Ross turned to look at her. 'And you could ultimately provide a transition out of sport and into something else if that's what they really want to do with their lives? Or transitions into sport if that's what they wanted.'

'Yes, exactly. They come first, and we'd be advocates for them.'

'It's got a lot of potential.'

'I'd start small, getting contacts and setting

things up. And when I do retire from rowing, I can devote more of my time to it on a regular basis.'

'You should talk to Sam about this. She'd be really interested in the idea, but she'd be the first to say that she doesn't have your killer instinct.'

'What?' Laurie aimed a play punch at his arm. 'You think I've got a killer instinct!'

'You know what I mean. You've got the audacity to go out and push people out of their comfort zone to make something work. Sam's got a lighter touch, she's no less committed but she'll kill you with kindness rather than running at you with a battering ram. It takes all sorts, and together you might be unstoppable.'

This was what Ross did so well. Putting people together. Seeing how different approaches might work in harmony instead of tugging against each other.

'Could I count on your support?' She hardly dared ask him. It would be a way of keeping one thread of contact with Ross.

'Always. If the clinic can help you in any way, you only have to call.'

That wasn't what she meant. The clinic could certainly help her, but it was Ross himself that she really wanted. Laurie hardly dared ask.

'What about you, Ross? Will you help me?'

He pressed his lips together, and Laurie shivered in the afternoon sunshine.

'I can't. You know the reasons why, and that it's not that I don't want to. If you do this it has to be something for yourself and the kids you want to help.'

'I'm planning on setting up a charity, not a dating agency. You want to help these kids too, I know you do.'

The reply was only half a joke. If Ross thought that this was her way of keeping in contact with him… It wasn't, it was something that she wanted to do. But if one of the by-products was that she *did* keep Ross on her mailing list, and maybe in her life as well, it was an idea that suddenly appealed to Laurie a great deal.

He nodded, and for a brief moment she let herself bask in the idea that her future might contain Ross.

'I do. But I'm sorry, Laurie, we can't do it together.'

CHAPTER FOURTEEN

ROSS STOOD IN the doorway of the gym, watching as Sam and Laurie led the mother and toddler exercise class. Sam had brought Timothy in to help and being a little older than most of the other children in the class he was taking his responsibilities seriously, standing next to his mother and reproducing the exercises she was teaching. Clearly they'd been practising together.

Laurie was having fun, too. She moved amongst the group, helping those who needed help and quietly correcting the posture of anyone not keeping their back straight. A little girl started to fret, and Laurie spoke to her mother and then picked her up.

A month ago, Ross wouldn't have believed what he was seeing. Laurie, smiling at the child on her hip, entertaining her so that her mother could exercise in peace. She was good with her too, bringing a smile to the little girl's face with almost no effort at all.

'This one works better with two...' Sam raised her voice in a broad hint, but Laurie seemed intent on sorting through the toybox with her new friend. 'Laurie!'

'Oh. Sorry...' Laurie brought the little girl back to the group, pulling a dismayed face. Her mother took her, telling her daughter that she could go back and play with Laurie as soon as they'd accomplished this exercise together.

Ross turned away.

He'd been thinking a lot about what she'd said the other day. It had sounded like an invitation, a way that they could keep in touch and explore the idea of continuing their relationship. Maybe even take it further... Every time he thought about the prospect, he felt intense happiness, coupled with physical yearning that almost stopped him in his tracks.

But watching her now... Laurie was growing and reaching out. Who knew what the future would bring for her, or whether she'd be changing her mind about not wanting a family of her own?

He could stop wondering now. Trying to think of ways that he might share his life with her. Because the one thing he *didn't* want to share with Laurie was the grief and heartache of wanting their own child and not being able to conceive. She deserved better than that.

By the time he heard a sound at the balcony doors, Ross had resigned himself to keeping their arrangement exactly as it was. There were only a few days to go before she was due to leave, and although they hadn't discussed a date, Laurie had been reducing her work at the clinic. Taking her into his arms made that prospect a great deal easier to bear because it was then that Ross lost sight of everything other than the kiss that would so surely follow.

'I've been thinking.' She kissed him with the kind of passion that told Ross that whatever she *had* been thinking he was going to like it.

'Uh-huh? You should do more of it.' He nodded towards the bed. Dinner could wait.

'Not that.' She nudged his ribs with her elbow. 'Or I should probably say not *just* that.'

Ross chuckled, stepping back and holding up his arms in a gesture of surrender. 'Okay. So you've been thinking about sex and something else. I'll leave you to lead with whichever you reckon ought to go first.'

She walked into the kitchen, peering into the oven to see what was cooking and nodding her head in approval. Then she sat down at the kitchen table while Ross poured them each a glass of wine.

'I thought I'd just say it....' She grinned a little nervously and took a sip of her wine.

'That's always a plan.' Ross sat down opposite her, leaning across the table to take her hands between his. Whatever it was seemed to be bugging her, and a faint pulse of concern started to beat at his consciousness.

Laurie took a breath, which made the pulse beat louder. Then flashed him a smile that drove it away for a moment.

'I know you have concerns about continuing our relationship, Ross. But I want you to know that if you're up for giving it a try, that's what I'd really like to do.'

Warmth and pleasure drained from the moment as a challenging abyss opened up beneath him. Only Laurie could tip his world so completely. Ross's shock must have shown on his face because she was staring at him now.

'Say something. Please...'

He squeezed her fingers in what he hoped was a reassuring gesture. 'There's nothing I'd like more, sweetheart. But I don't think we can do that.'

Maybe she'd leave it there, and not make him go into details. And maybe not. Ross reminded himself that one of the things he adored about

Laurie was her ability to say exactly what was on her mind.

'Why? Is this your way of telling me that you don't want me?'

Ross closed his eyes, rubbing his hands across his face. 'I don't think there'll ever be a time when I don't want you, Laurie. What I'm saying is that you and I can never have a family, and I won't ask you to give that possibility up for me.'

She reddened a little, her jaw setting in an adorably stubborn tilt. 'What if I don't care about that? What if I…' She hesitated briefly, before continuing in almost a whisper, 'What if I love you?'

Ross knew he loved her, too. It was the only thing that explained the deep sadness spreading through him at the thought of not spending his life with her. But he also knew it didn't matter. He could give Laurie his love, but she deserved so much more. Saying it would only draw out this agony.

'Do you even know what you'll be doing this time next year? What you'll care about? Because if we stay together, I'm not sure that I can let you go.'

Laurie sprang to her feet, pacing the kitchen. He loved her restless energy too…

'Then don't, Ross. Don't let me go.'

'Are you telling me that you can be happy with no prospect of ever having children?'

She stilled suddenly, pressing her lips together and staring at him. Ross could feel his heart hardening. It was the only way that he could bring himself to push Laurie away.

'Can't you just trust me, Ross? Can't you believe that I can accept that?'

'I trust you. Life's the thing I really don't trust…'

'Oh!' She flung her hands in the air in an expression of frustration. 'We're in control of our own lives, aren't we? Whatever happened to not giving up?'

'And whatever happened to facing facts?' Ross could feel his brow tightening into a frown. 'Or to making the best of what you have, for that matter?'

'Fine.' Anger flared in her beautiful eyes. 'You make the best of what you have, then. Don't give a second thought to anything else because it's just too much trouble to try for it.'

That stung. All the feelings about his marriage came flooding back. Alice's reproachful looks when she'd found that he'd failed her again that month.

'Grow up, Laurie. You might feel that you can push yourself and achieve all you want out of life, and maybe you're right. But none of that gives you the right to expect me to achieve the impossible.'

Her eyes widened in outrage. 'That's not what I'm saying, Ross. I'm telling you that we take what we have now and make something good from it.'

'And I'm telling you that we can't.'

Her lip began to quiver. If she cried, Ross wasn't sure that he'd be able to let her go, but Laurie pulled herself together suddenly, straightening her back and shooting him that blank look that denied him any access to her feelings.

'We're done, then.' She murmured the words, turning and walking out of the kitchen. Ross jumped as the front door of the apartment banged closed behind her.

It should have been an easy equation. Two suitcases in, two suitcases out. It was the way Laurie always travelled, never bringing home any more than she'd taken with her. The equation wasn't working this time.

There were her clothes. They weren't too much of a problem, although there were two T-shirts with the clinic logo on them and the fruits of a shopping trip with Ross, a pair of sandals that she'd bought to replace those she'd waterlogged, and a skirt she'd liked that he'd encouraged her to buy. They'd fit easily. The cork from the bottle of champagne that had been so much fun to drink, and which Ross had cut and inserted a coin into for luck, didn't take up much space either. Maybe she should just throw that away as it stirred up too many memories, but she couldn't bear to. She had so little of him to keep already.

There were so many other things, though. The comic strip that Adam had drawn for her. The two yellow feathers that had fluttered out of her T-shirt when she'd pulled it over her head on the evening of the school sports day, pressed carefully inside the programme like flowers between the leaves of a book. The rowing cap that Tamara had given her, which Laurie had promised to wear at her next competition, and the folder full of useful reading matter that Sam had presented her with when Laurie had suggested they collaborate on ideas for a new charity. Drawings from the kids at the mother and toddler class.

Then there were the books that Ross had taken from his shelves for her to read. They were a little easier. She'd only read a few of them, but she would leave them all behind, because there would be no opportunity to return them later.

'You know it's over when she starts to separate her books and music from yours...'

Grant had said that when one of the stream of girlfriends he'd had before he was married had left. The thought hit home now with a new appreciation of how incredibly sad the process of leaving someone was. She'd never let a relationship get far enough before now to exchange anything that needed to be returned.

She carried the books through to the sitting room, feeling tears prick at the sides of her eyes. Laurie wiped them away. This was a new kind of pain and it was hard to pretend she didn't feel it.

This was by no means the first time they'd argued, two strong characters who enjoyed the clash of wills and liked the ultimate reconciliation even better. But this time it was different. Ross was right, and at the same time a little bit wrong. He'd said he couldn't give her what she needed, but in truth it was Laurie who couldn't give him what he needed. She couldn't make him believe that stepping out into uncharted waters with her wasn't going to lead to disaster. Her love wasn't enough for that.

Now she could cry if the wanted to, and maybe it would ease the suffocating pressure in her chest. But clearly she didn't deserve the relief of tears, and they wouldn't come. She'd just helped destroy the best thing that had ever happened to her and there was no going back. Leaving might be the right thing to do, but it felt that this loss would overshadow everything from now on.

Ross had waited for the timer on the oven to ping, and tipped this evening's dinner straight into a freezer dish, abandoning it to cool. Slinging himself into an armchair, he glared at the wall.

Why hadn't he fallen on his knees and begged Laurie to stay?

Because it would have been wrong, that was why. There was no more talking to be done, no more making love and no goodbyes. This was the end, and going back now would only postpone the inevitable and make it worse. If the rest of his life was going to be lived without Laurie, he should accept it and get on with it.

But despite himself, Ross sat up late, brooding in the darkness and waking early the next morning to find his neck stiff and his leg numb from falling asleep on the sofa.

The sound of a car outside on the gravel drive took him over to the front window. Laurie had been waiting for the taxi, and the driver helped her load her suitcases into the boot.

Ross closed his eyes. This was the right

thing to do, but he wouldn't watch her go. All the same, his lips formed the words.

Goodbye, my love. Be happy.

'Ross!'

There was only one person who could lend that note of exasperation to Sam's voice. An instinctive smile jumped to Ross's lips and then he remembered, yet again, that Laurie had gone. It had been almost a month now, and that hollow feeling of loss never seemed to get any better.

He took a breath, waving Sam to a seat and leaning back in his own office chair. Sam and Laurie had been working together on the new initiative for teenagers, and he'd helped Sam as much as he could. It hurt when Sam talked about Laurie but this was his only remaining thread of contact and he held onto it greedily.

'What's on your mind, Sam?'

'I so love that woman…'

Yeah. He could relate to that.

'…and she's driving me crazy.'

The chance would be a fine thing. Laurie could drive him crazy any time she liked, but Ross knew that she wouldn't be back.

'What's up?' He tried to focus on Sam.

'You know the swimmer, Phil Jacques? Of course you do, everyone does. Laurie's only gone and roped him in for a round-table discussion about sports training for teenagers.'

'That's good, isn't it? It's exactly what you need—a few household names on board.'

'It's fabulous. But you know when it is?'

'I reckon you're about to tell me.'

'Two weeks' time. At the conference in Birmingham that we were thinking of going to.'

'Okay…' Ross had been planning to spend a couple of days in Birmingham in two weeks to take in the conference and visit some prospective patients there. He wasn't quite sure how he felt about sharing a city with Laurie, but his heart knew how to react. It started to pump wildly.

'They're going to do it in front of an audience and it'll be recorded for radio. Laurie's asked some other guests and she's going to use this as an opportunity to announce the new initiative. She's done all this in less than a month.'

That's my girl.

'You know there's no stopping her when she decides to do something. So…what's the problem? Aren't you pleased?'

'I'm delighted. Only…she wants me to chair the discussion.' Sam shot him an agonised look.

Sam was the best physiotherapist he knew, and she was great with her patients. She had more than enough knowledge to chair any discussion about the project that she and Laurie had been working on, and Ross guessed that this was Laurie's way of giving Sam the credit she deserved for all the hard work she'd done. The only trouble was that Laurie had underestimated how shy Sam was when it came to public speaking.

'I suppose…you couldn't focus on the fact that you deserve this, could you? Or that you're just the right person to do it, and you'd be great?'

'No. Ross, I really couldn't. In front of an auditorium full of people? Recorded for the radio?' Sam pressed her lips together, obviously trying not to think about it. 'You couldn't do it, could you?'

'You mean go along there and take all the credit for your work? I'm not entirely comfortable with that, no.' Ross wasn't comfortable with gatecrashing Laurie's discussion either. He wasn't sure which would be worse, finding himself in an argument with her or being on the receiving end of her blank, professional stare.

'But you've really helped us. You gave me that long list of contacts and wrote introduction letters to all of them. You deserve a bit of credit for that.'

'I'm just helping out. You and Laurie are the ones steering this.'

'But Laurie can't do it. This whole thing is a fantastic opportunity for her to be able to speak about her own experience of the pressures that can face teenagers in sport, and she can't do that and chair the discussion at the same time. Please, Ross…'

He had to suggest something. 'All right. Let's break it down, Sam. What in particular are you most concerned about?'

Sam took a moment to think. 'Well, for starters, there's what to wear. Then what to say. When to say it, whether to ask questions or not, or whether I should just introduce people and let them get on with it…' She took a breath, and Ross used the opportunity to jump in.

'That'll do for starters. Can Jamie help with the what-to-wear-part? Go through your wardrobe with you?'

'Jamie? You're joking, of course. He says that I always look nice, so anything would do.'

'I'd be inclined to agree with him. That's no help, is it?'

'No, Ross. It's really no help at all.'

'All right. Well, moving on, have you asked Laurie what she wants you to say?'

'She said to steer the discussion. Get the best out of everyone.'

Ross was on firmer ground here. He knew exactly what Laurie meant. 'All right, so that's asking questions. We'll get a list of the guests and work out some questions for each of them, shall we?'

He was pretty sure that Sam knew which points needed to be emphasised, it was just a matter of sitting her down, somehow stopping her from panicking and getting the information out of her. If he and Jamie joined forces, that would be a piece of cake.

'Oh, would you? But when do I ask them?'

'We'll practise. We can get a few people from the clinic together, and we'll have some discussions. How about that?'

Sam nodded. 'Yes, that would be good too. But what on earth am I going to wear?'

Ross suspected that was Sam's biggest problem. If she could go in knowing that she looked like a million dollars, she'd be much more confident. Even if it *was* radio.

'I think I've got an idea. Remember Anita Lower?' Sam looked at him blankly. 'Compression of the third and fourth thoracic vertebrae.'

'Oh, yes I remember now. Nice lady. In such terrible pain. She's a friend of yours, isn't she?'

'Yes, and she always asks after you whenever I see her. She really appreciated all that you did for her. We're overdue a lunch together, and I want you to come along too. As you know, Anita works as an image consultant for a number of the big TV companies.'

Sam stared at him. 'Would she…? That's far too much to ask, Ross.'

'No, it's not. Anita's told me more than once that you turned her life around, and I know she'd be delighted to see you again. We'll go shopping and…' Ross waved his hand in the air to indicate that whatever it was that Anita did, she'd do it for Sam.

'Shopping!' Sam was all smiles now. 'Do you think I can do this?'

'My honest opinion… Yes, I think you'll ace it.'

'And Laurie's going to be there, of course.' A shadow fell over Sam's face suddenly. 'You'll come, won't you?'

He wanted to go, so badly. Just to see Laurie again, even if it was at a distance in the crowded auditorium of the hotel conference centre. To see her life moving forward, because that was the only thing he had to hold onto. That Laurie should be happy, because he couldn't imagine himself being truly happy again.

'I'll have to see.'

'See what? The same thing that Laurie was

going to have to see when I suggested she invite you along? I know you two were close, Ross...' Sam turned the corners of her mouth down. 'You argued, didn't you?'

There was no point in denying it. Sam wasn't blind, and she was a good friend. She'd navigated a difficult situation with her customary ease, allowing Ross to support the initiative in many small ways, without ever asking why he did it through her and not by contacting Laurie himself.

'It's complicated, Sam.'

'I dare say it is. You know what's really ironic?'

A feeling of irony wasn't one of the emotions he'd experienced yet. He may as well, the others were a lot more draining.

'What's that?'

'I've known you a long time, but this is the first time that you've ever thought that *complicated* was a reason not to do something. Laurie's just the same. The more complicated and challenging something is, the better she likes it.'

He shouldn't ask. It wasn't fair to Sam, but he couldn't help it.

'How is she?'

Sam considered the question for a moment. 'I know you need to know, so I'll tell you. Just this once because I'm not going to be a go-between.' She paused, looking for Ross's assent, and he nodded.

'She's well. Her hip is in really good shape and she's getting back to full fitness now. She's working every waking hour, just as you are...' Sam shot him a knowing look. 'I see the same thing in both of you. Whatever happened between you broke both your hearts.'

Ross nodded. Sam was looking at him expectantly. Taking a deep breath, he said, 'She told me she loved me, that she wanted us to try to build a relationship together.'

Sam smiled sadly. 'And you said no.' It wasn't a question. He nodded again. 'Why?'

'Because I can't do it again, I can't be responsible for ruining someone else's dreams.'

'You weren't responsible for ruining Alice's dreams, Ross. She was wrong to put that on you. But you're wrong to push Laurie away. Clearly she knows about your fertility issue and yet she still wanted to be with you. You're denying yourself a chance at happiness—don't! Opportunities like this don't come along every day, when it's there in front of you, telling you you're loved and wanted? That's when you grab it with both hands. Now, the question is, what are you going to do about it?'

Ross stared dumbly at Sam, who was a little

pink-cheeked now. Clearly this had been on her mind for a while, and now she'd put it into words Sam rose from her seat and walked out of his office.

He stood, looking out at the lake. It was the same view that usually helped him think through any difficulty that arose, but right now it wasn't helping.

He'd accepted what life had offered him and made the best he could of it. Now he had to go out on a limb to get what he really wanted.

CHAPTER FIFTEEN

LAURIE LOOKED WONDERFUL. She was wearing a cream, silky blouse with dark trousers, and the flaming red of her hair lifted the outfit from sensible to incredibly sexy.

She was nervous, though, Ross could see that. Even from this distance, right at the back of the auditorium, it was obvious that she was reading a prepared statement about the new initiative and she stumbled a couple of times. But Sam was magnificent. She gave Laurie an excited smile and asked the question that Ross had primed her with, the one he knew that Laurie would want to answer. Then Laurie started to loosen up a bit.

He mentally ticked off the points she made in his head. When she missed one, Sam came to the rescue and asked an appropriate question. All the work that he and Anita had done with Sam had been worth it.

The presentation finished to loud applause,

and people began to crowd around Laurie. He should go. But Ross didn't move from his seat, wanting to see her at the centre of everyone's attention for just a little while longer.

He saw Sam scanning the audience as the lights in the auditorium went up. The look on her face and the impatient movement of her hand signified that he should be down on the stage, congratulating Laurie. Ross shook his head. Now wasn't the time.

But Laurie had turned, looking at Sam and then following her gaze. Her head tipped up towards him and for a moment they were the only two people in the crowded space. Then that cool, emotionless look that told Ross that Laurie was struggling with her emotions as much as he was.

He really did have to go now. He should leave her there, in the limelight, to do what she'd come here to do. Ross dragged his gaze away from the stage, looking for the nearest exit.

Ross was here. Laurie felt sick with excitement and then horrified that he'd got up from his seat and left the auditorium as soon as she'd seen him. It wasn't like him to turn away from a confrontation, however awkward, and Laurie tried not to go through all the reasons why he might have done and concentrate on the conversations she was having with the people around her.

It all took a while. There were questions, expressions of support, and a few pleas for help. The contact sheets they'd drawn up were filling fast, and that was exactly what she and Sam had hoped for. There was no way Laurie could have followed Ross, and even if she had, she didn't know what to say to him. Tell him about the pain of being apart from him? That she loved him? Or just lie to him and tell him that she'd succeeded without him and that she didn't need him?

Finally, it was just her and Sam, standing on the stage together, watching the outside broadcast team pack up their equipment. Laurie hugged Sam, and they walked back to the reception area of the hotel that was hosting the conference, where Jamie was waiting with Timothy. Laurie made a smiling excuse when Jamie asked her to join them for a spot of lunch and retreated to the lift, breathing a sigh of relief as the doors closed, leaving her alone.

She needed time to think. Ross was here and that *had* to mean something. Her hotel room on the fourteenth floor had the dual advantage of being somewhere to consider her next move and also somewhere that he could find her if he wanted to…

Laurie kicked off her shoes, deciding that she wouldn't explore the possibility that Ross would ask in Reception for her room number. He'd left the auditorium when she'd seen him, and he clearly wasn't in any hurry to see her. She dialled room service and ordered coffee.

'That was quick…' The knock had sounded after only a couple of minutes and Laurie had pulled the door open, expecting to see the room-service waiter outside.

Ross. Looking just as deliciously handsome as ever. More so. Laurie wasn't a connoisseur of men in suits, but he wore his very well. Darkly immaculate and thrillingly dangerous sprang to mind.

'You're waiting for someone?' The gesture of his hand indicated that he could go away and come back later.

'No! Well, yes, but it's only room service.' If she had to grab him and strong-arm him into the room, she was prepared to do it.

But that wasn't necessary. His gaze met hers, and that gorgeous synchronicity of movement that they'd always shared kicked in. She stepped back from the door at the same moment that Ross stepped forward. Nothing else mattered now, just that they were both breathing the same air.

'The presentation was great. Inspiring. You've worked hard.'

Was that what he'd come to say? Laurie swallowed down her disappointment. 'Thanks. Sam saved my life a couple of times. How long have you been here?'

'I arrived late last night.'

'And when were you thinking of leaving?'

'Not until I'd spoken to you.'

The whole world seemed suddenly bathed in light. And then she was in his arms. How that had happened wasn't entirely clear to Laurie, but she didn't care. She heard the door slam as Ross kicked it closed behind him, and snuggled into his embrace, breathing in his scent.

'Laurie… I've missed you so much.'

'Not as much as I missed you…'

'You want to make a competition out of it?' He smiled down at her and all the things that she wanted to say to him were lost in the gentle, flickering fire of his eyes.

'Yes. Let's do that.'

He kissed her, with all the passion and longing that she felt. Brilliant happiness robbed Laurie of anything other than the thought that he was here and holding her in his arms. And when she kissed him back she felt the sweet response of his body against hers.

Now all she could think of was the bed, and the few yards between them and it. Maybe they wouldn't even make it. Passion was clawing at her and Ross's kisses were driving everything else from her head. If she had only these moments with him, she would take them and deal with the consequences later.

She slipped his jacket from his shoulders, and Ross shrugged it off. Slowly, deliberately, she loosened his tie. Making him wait while the passion built between them, even more heady than it had ever been. He pulled her back against him, kissing her with a hunger that made her head spin.

Another knock on the door, and a voice announcing that this time it really *was* room service, made them spring apart guiltily. Laurie opened the door, feeling in her pocket for a tip, and then grabbed the tray, dumping it onto the credenza before she turned back to face Ross.

Gone. The moment was gone. She could see it in his face.

'Second thoughts?'

He pressed his lips together. 'It's not what I came for, Laurie. I came to talk.'

'Okay. I'll ask them to bring another cup…' She made for the door, wondering if the waiter had disappeared into the lift yet, but Ross caught her arm.

'I don't need coffee. What I *do* need is to tell you that I love you. If you can forgive me, and love me too, then we need to sit down and work out what we're going to do about that.'

There was only one cup. That didn't matter, she was just concentrating on irrelevant details because she couldn't get her head around the enormity of what Ross had just said. Laurie resisted the temptation to throw herself into his arms because he was right. They needed to talk about this. She poured the coffee with a shaking hand, taking a sip and then handing the cup to him.

'I love you, too. I'm sorry I left without saying goodbye.'

'Don't be. I drove you away, and…it was wrong of me. I couldn't see a way for us to be together and I thought it was for the best. I'm sorry.' Ross took a sip of coffee and handed the cup back to her, sitting down on the bed.

'Now we've got that over with…' Laurie sat down next to him, her heart thumping wildly. 'What are we going to do now?'

Everything depended on his answer. Laurie had thought about it and hadn't been able to find a plan that might work. She had to trust that Ross would be able to provide the answers that she couldn't, and suddenly that didn't seem so impossible.

'I know that I'm not a good prospect for anyone…' He stumbled over the words, and Laurie laid her hand on his.

'You just happen to be the one that I want. I've no desire to change that, even if I could.'

'I can't change it either. You're the only woman I'll ever want, and I love you with all my heart. The thought that you could love me too is what's given me the courage to come here and ask what I shouldn't of you…'

'Ask, Ross. I want to hear it.'

He nodded, taking the cup from her hands and laying it aside. Then he fell to one knee in front of her.

'Laurie, I want to take your hopes and dreams and make them happen for you. Everything you ever wanted, or will want, because they're more important than anything to me. Will you take mine, and hold them in trust for me?'

She saw it. Ross's way forward, a clear road that led to their future together. He might not be able to trust in life, but he knew that he could trust her.

'Give me your dreams. I'll take care of them and I won't let them hurt or disappoint you again. I'll give you mine, because I know that they're safe in your hands.'

'You're sure?' He blinked, as if he couldn't quite believe what he was hearing.

'Yes, I'm sure! Listen to what I'm saying to you for once, will you?'

Ross grinned. 'Okay. I'm listening. If I promise to always listen, always love you and try my best to make you happy, will you marry me?'

Tears filled her eyes and Laurie made no effort to brush them away. She didn't need to any more. Leaning forward, she flung her arms around his neck.

'Yes, Ross. I'll marry you.'

She felt his chest heave with emotion. Gently he disentangled himself from her arms. 'Close your eyes. I'm not letting you get away this time…'

She squeezed her eyes shut. There was a moment's pause and then Laurie felt him slip a ring on her finger. Then his lips were on hers as he kissed her. She kissed him back, holding onto him tightly.

'You can look at it now…' His lips brushed hers as he murmured the words.

'Is it nice?' She clasped her fingers together behind his neck. 'Feels heavy…'

Ross chuckled. 'I spent a while choosing it.

Nothing was going to really be good enough for you, but I got the best I could find.'

'Then I love it. I'll look at it in a minute. Right now, I can't take my eyes off you, because it's been far too long since I've seen you.'

'Yeah. You're stuck with me now, that's not going to happen again.'

The world had shifted, and it was a different place now. Laurie stared at him, tears running down her cheeks, and Ross gently brushed them away, before folding her in his arms.

'Do you feel different?'

'Yeah, I feel different.' Ross chuckled quietly. 'It's everything, Laurie. Your love and mine, your dreams and mine. Nothing's going to stop us now.'

EPILOGUE

Four years later

THIS YEAR THEY'D picked Munich. The same hotel suite that Ross had booked for the World Championships three years ago. With the same hot tub to luxuriate in together, and the same stunning view over the city.

'How have I been doing as caretaker?' Ross handed Laurie a glass of champagne. It was the same question he asked every year, on the anniversary of the day they'd given their dreams to each other for safekeeping.

'Beautifully.' Laurie smiled up at him. 'Each year I wonder how you're going to surpass the last, but you always manage it.'

'More stamina than you expected?'

'A lot more.' She leaned into his arms, stretching to kiss him. 'I never thought anyone could love me so well. Or be such a great rowing coach.'

'I just cheered you on. Win or lose.'

'That's what made all the difference. And you made a very good job of cheering the last time we were here.' Ross had been hoarse for a week afterwards.

'It was worth it. I'll never forget the look on your face when you stepped up onto the podium and received your gold medal.' He bent to kiss her. 'Or the one when you made my dream come true and married me.'

'Hey! Are you pinching my dreams, Ross? A girl's wedding day is supposed to be *her* dream.'

Ross chuckled. 'Too bad. It was my dream as well. You can share, can't you?'

'With you? Everything.'

That was the way things were now. The new extension to the clinic, which was going to be a training centre for young athletes and house the charity that Sam and Laurie managed together, had been Laurie's idea, but Ross had put his heart into it as well. He'd taken care of her dreams and adopted them as his own.

A sound came from the bedroom and Ross looked round. 'Seems our favourite dream has woken up. I'll go and get her.'

Laurie never tired of watching him with their daughter. When she followed him to the doorway, she saw Ross lifting Penelope out of her cot, still wrapped in the baby quilt her grandmother had made for her. This was the best dream of all, the one in a thousand chance that had happened when they'd least expected it.

'Daddy…' Penelope knew just how to twist her father around her little finger. All it took was that one word.

'Hey, there, Penelope. You want to come and see what we're doing?'

'Daddy… Want play.'

Ross caught his breath. 'You want to play? With your bear?' He picked the stuffed bear up from beside the cot and Penelope pushed it away.

'Want play…'

'With me?' Ross made a funny face and Penelope laughed, her small fingers reaching for him.

'Did you hear that? Her first sentence. Almost…' His voice was a little hoarse, as if he had a lump in his throat.

'It sounded like a sentence to me.' Laurie allowed herself a smile. She'd been repeating the words to Penelope for a couple of weeks now, and finally the little girl had decided to use them herself. Her timing was impeccable.

'You haven't been teaching her to say that, have you?' Ross shot Laurie a suspicious look.

'Me? Would I do such a thing?'

He chuckled, holding out his hand to pull her close. 'You most definitely would. And I love you for it.'

'I love you, too, Ross. I have all my dreams right here.' She snuggled against him. The warm smell of his body, along with Penelope's gorgeous baby scent, enveloped her in a cocoon of happiness.

He kissed her cheek, a warm reminder of what tonight would hold after Penelope was asleep again. A crazy, unlikely thought began to form…

'Do you ever wonder? Whether a one in thousand chance might happen twice? We could try IVF this time…'

Ross chuckled 'Turning my world upside down *once* wasn't enough for you? You think I can survive a second time?'

'It was the first time I've ever seen you stunned into silence.' Those moments, when they'd stared at the pregnancy test together, and when she'd wiped tears from his eyes with shaking fingers, had been among the best of her life. They were enough, but Laurie had learned how to want more, in the face of knowing it might never happen.

'IVF's an option. Although I much prefer the traditional way.' A wicked grin hovered on his lips. 'Do you reckon that's one thousand times? Or one thousand full nights…?'

'I reckon nights. Statistically it could be a lot more.' Laurie shivered with pleasure at the thought. 'The journey's well worth it, even if we never get there.'

'My thoughts entirely.' He kissed her again, and she felt Penelope's small body wriggling between them.

'Daddy want… Want to play, Daddy.'

'You want *to* play, Penelope?' He chuckled. 'That's my girl. Unless I'm very much mistaken, she's just used an infinitive…'

'In that case, we'd better go and play with her immediately.' Laurie went to move, but Ross held her tight against him.

'I want to make another bargain with you. That we never stop dreaming.'

They'd always have more to do together, and Laurie couldn't wait to find out what would come next for them.

'It's a deal, Ross. Always.'

* * * * *

If you enjoyed this story, check out these other great reads from Annie Claydon

Greek Island Fling to Forever
The Best Man and the Bridesmaid
Healing the Vet's Heart
A Rival to Steal Her Heart

All available now!